TIM MEYER

EVIL EPOCH
PRESS

69

Published by Evil Epoch Press

Edited by Jenny Adams

Cover Art by James "Toe" Keen

This book is a work of fiction. Names, characters, businesses, organizations, places, events, and incidents either are the product of the author's imagination or are used fictitiously. Any resemblance to actual person, living or dead, events or locales is entirely coincidental.

International Standard Book Number (ISBN):
978-1-7323993-3-4

Printed in the United States of America

AUTHOR'S NOTE

Although some of the things you'll find in this novel were researched, I have taken certain liberties regarding the CDC and their operating procedures.
That is all. Enjoy the show.

– T.M.

"There had stood a great house in the centre of the gardens, where now was left only that fragment of ruin. This house had been empty for a great while; years before his—the ancient man's—birth. It was a place shunned by the people of the village, as it had been shunned by their fathers before them. There were many things said about it, and all were of evil. No one ever went near it, either by day or night. In the village it was a synonym of all that is unholy and dreadful."

– William Hope Hodgson,
The House on the Borderland

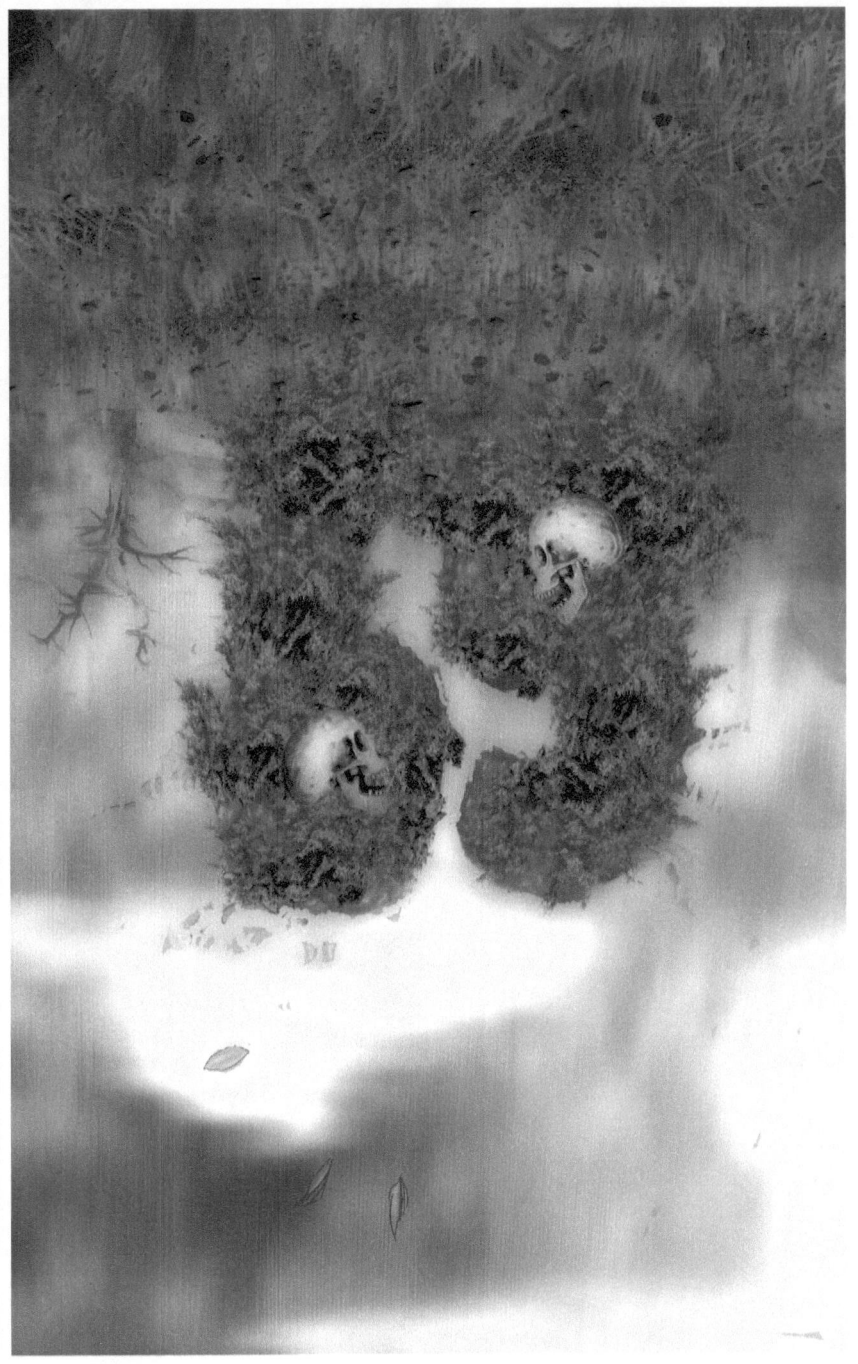

1

PETRIFIED FACES. OPEN mouths. Unheard screams. Stiff limbs. A room full of dead bodies that weren't really dead, just frozen, fixed standing, sitting, walking. Amanda Guerrero had never seen anything like it, not in her ten years working for the CDC. Acute flaccid myelitis, Huntington's disease, Batten disease; none of it came close to the symptoms she'd documented here.

She paced the common room of the Spring Lake Assisted Living facility, surveying the situation and trying to figure out where to begin, how to dissect and comprehend what her eyes were allowing her to see. And more importantly, how to divvy up the tasks at hand.

Her team—all two of them—filed into the room. Barnes was already scribbling on his notepad. He stopped when he noticed the faces of the elderly, every resident whose age had hit the magical number of sixty-nine, whose bodies had stiffened and became corpse-like at some point throughout the early morning.

"Jesus Christ," he said, his pen stopping mid-stroke.

Understatement of the century, Amanda thought, clicking on her flashlight and peeking into the mouth of one of the sixty-niners—a woman with short curly gray hair and more wrinkles than a crumpled bed sheet. Nothing seemed out of the ordinary with her *(medically speaking),* other than she was frozen still, unmoving, and her eyes remained open despite her dead-like

11

state, staring into a place somewhere beyond Spring Lake. At first glance, one would suggest the woman had died sitting up; in fact, that was exactly the diagnosis given by the good people at Spring Lake when they had discovered seven of their guests, the only sixty-nine-year-olds out of the total one-hundred-and-fifty patients, motionless and utterly catatonic. A local doctor—a well-respected physician who was high on scholarly merits and short on common sense—dropped in to check out the peculiar claims made by the facility's director, Kim Charon, and was utterly surprised to discover the patients *weren't* dead. Not really. Dr. Ken Lacey, as he'd introduced himself over the phone, had felt their pulses and listened to the slow beats of their hearts. The sixty-niners were alive, indeed, though just barely by the doctor's estimation.

It's like they are frozen in some sort of... catatonic state, he had told Amanda during their conversation. *I think it may be viral.*

He hadn't elaborated on his second statement but had suggested Amanda and her team should make the trek to New Jersey because it was unlike anything he'd ever seen—or heard of—before. He had also added the situation *freaked him the hell out.*

Amanda turned to Barnes who was now leaning in the face of an old man, shining his pocket light in his open, staring eyes.

"Barnes," she said, adjusting her surgeon's mask. "Grab Phelps and start collecting saliva samples. I want them analyzed ASAP."

Phelps, who'd heard her name being called, reentered the room.

Barnes had hardly reacted to his boss's request. He was too fixed on the old man, the inexplicable nature of his static state.

"Barnes," she repeated, still failing to capture his attention. *"Barnes."*

He snapped out of it, clicked off the light, and rose to a standing position. Alert. "What's up?"

"You and Phelps. Saliva samples. Now."

Phelps came over and grabbed his arm, helping him away from his current distraction.

Finally tearing his gaze away from the old man, Barnes nodded. "You got it, boss." He left the room and exited through the front door, heading back to the rental van. Phelps tagged along behind him. Amanda watched them go.

A few bodies that weren't frozen to their seats or rooted to the floor continued to pace the room. One of them belonged to the facility's director, Kim Charon. There were two nurses whose names Amanda hadn't caught. Two others, *lawyers* Amanda suspected, also walked around the common area between the front lobby and the hallway that contained the residents' living quarters. Amanda hadn't been introduced to them either, though, she was pretty sure Kim wouldn't involve the suits until *after* they traced the source of the virus, if indeed a virus was what they were dealing with.

What else could it be? She wasn't sure, didn't have the slightest clue, but she echoed Dr. Lacey's off-the-record statement all the same—*it was freaky.*

Those aged sixty-nine, seven in total, were as stiff as petrified wood, stuck in various positions, as if they'd gazed directly into the eyes of the fabled villain Medusa and turned to stone. There were two women in the corner sitting at a small table, each of them with a seemingly untouched cup of tea before them. One had her head cocked back, mouth open, eyes tilted toward the ceiling, looking like she'd seen something up there that had given her quite the shock. The five other victims around the facility appeared in similar fashion, each looking surprised at something they'd seen. Some were more expressive than others, but Amanda could see beyond the story their faces told—it was their eyes that truly gave them away. Whatever they'd witnessed before succumbing to that unnatural state of inertia—it wasn't pleasant. One male, who'd been wearing a flat cap atop his curly, so-gray-it's-white hair, was tilting his head to the side, his eyes halfway closed as if he were about to doze off on his feet. His mouth was slightly open, forming the beginnings of a startled expression.

Amanda made her way across the common room, over to a sixty-niner sporting a cane. He seemed to have been heading toward the hallway when the sickness had overcome him. She directed the light into his left eye, watched the pupil shrink under the bright intrusion.

Reacting to light just like he would if he was awake. She wondered if they *were* awake behind their masks of inactivity. If they could see. Hear. Process everything that was happening around them. Generate thoughts. She wondered if *they* knew what was happening to them. If they understood.

Freaky.

She gripped the man's left arm. It was as hard as stone. His skin was cold, as if he'd been locked inside a walk-in freezer for the last few hours. *As if he were a corpse,* Amanda thought. Poking the man's chest, she found it as hard as the arm. A solid wall of muscle and bone. She couldn't help but think of Medusa again, the nest of snakes atop the monster's head. She wanted to test a theory, a quick hypothesis, but she wasn't sure if the lawyers would approve. *Screw it,* she told herself and went ahead anyway. Those weasels weren't running the show; she was in charge and she wasn't about to let a couple of clueless suits influence her ability to do her job.

She pushed the old man, gently shoved his right shoulder hard enough to dislodge him from his place under ordinary circumstances. When he didn't budge, she tested her strength against other parts of his body, his chest and back, using a little more force with each attempt. Again, the elderly man, who'd gotten around the facility with the assistance of a cane, could not be moved. He didn't waver so much as an inch. Didn't teeter, didn't bend. His skin didn't dimple when she pressed on his flesh. He remained there like a statue, one constructed of sturdy concrete.

"Should you be doing that?" asked one of the lawyerly types. He wore sunglasses, rose-lensed aviators, and had combed his thinning hair over to one side. Holding his briefcase as if it weighed as much as he could handle, he shot Amanda a stern look. She got the impression he was a man who rarely smiled, not even when he was charging a client two-fifty an hour to pencil some meaningless paperwork. "I mean, should we really be touching them when we don't know what's wrong with them? What if they're contagious or something?"

Amanda eyed him and arched her back, stretching her vertebrae. "What's your name? Don't think we've had the pleasure of meeting. Officially, that is."

The lawyer looked to his partner, then to Kim Charon as if asking her permission to speak. If she gave it, she did so silently. "Name's Hatterman."

Amanda glanced over at the other suit.

"Hart," he said. "Jim Hart." He was smaller than the other lawyer by a head, and his voice came out low, matching his stature.

"Pleasure to meet the both of you," Amanda told them. "We're not going to have any problems here, are we?"

Kim stepped forward. "No, of course not. They're only here to address any legal issues concerning our guests. That's all."

Amanda wriggled her eyebrows and ran her tongue between her teeth. "Sure thing. Just doing their jobs."

"Exactly."

"Good. And I'm trying to do mine." She nodded at Hatterman. "How else am I going to find out what happened here unless I run a few preliminary assessments? How can I run tests without touching them?"

Hatterman coughed into his fist. "I was just simply suggesting we shouldn't touch anything unless we know what we're dealing with."

Amanda pulled on the elastic band of her glove, allowing the rubber to slap against her wrist with an audible pop. The sound echoed across the room, the noise as effective as telling the lawyer to step back and fuck his own face-hole. Which was what she had wanted to say but had held her tongue. "I'm wearing my protection, Mr. Hatterman. Are you?"

Hatterman, who hadn't put on the mask he'd been handed despite Amanda's suggestion, turned his eyes to the paper protective dangling around his neck and, like a brat who thought he owned all the answers, reluctantly placed the mask over his face.

"What do you think has happened here?" asked Kim, as she made her way across the room, over to where the old man was hunched, frozen mid-stride. Once there, the director poked him with her forefinger just as Amanda had, only with a lot less pressure. She didn't seem to like the feeling of his rock-solid muscle and retracted her finger immediately, as if she'd placed it on a hot burner.

"Too early to tell. I'd like to run saliva samples, take blood, and get those results as soon as possible. Initial reaction—some sort of bacterial infection that's laid claim to their brains. There have been various reports of things like this happening in third-world countries— shit, just last year, a village in Africa was the subject of a 'zombie virus.' Of course, it didn't turn people into *actual* zombies, but the brain-eating bacteria did leave its victims walking around in a daze, drooling and unable to effectively communicate. I'm sure the fever had something to do with it, but—"

"Whoa, whoa, whoa," Kim said, closing her eyes and pumping one hand in the air. "What do you mean *bacteria?* This is the cleanest assisted living facility in the entire Garden State. There isn't any bacteria here. I make sure the nurses and aides wipe down each and every room twice a day. We vacuum, mop, disinfect every piece of furniture, every toilet. We pride ourselves on cleanliness." She closed her eyes and shook her head. "No, I won't accept that. It's impossible."

Amanda flashed an amused smile. "That very well may be, Ms. Charon."

"*Mrs.* Charon." She flashed her diamond ring, which sparkled magnificently under the room's bright LEDs.

"Mrs.," she corrected. Her smile faded into a cautious wince. "You may be the cleanest facility in the *country,* but that doesn't mean something like this can't happen. A visitor, a family member of one of your patients, could have flown in yesterday from halfway around the world, having contracted the disease and bringing it back with them."

"*Guests.*"

"I'm sorry?"

"We prefer to call our residents *guests*, dear."

"Yeah, guests. Anyway, who's to say one of their family members didn't catch something on vacation or while volunteering in some less fortunate region of the world? There's no telling right now, exactly, what happened. Which is why we're here. Which is why we're going to run a few tests, take a few samples, and hopefully get to the bottom of this anomaly. The good thing is that no one seems to be in immediate danger. Everyone has a pulse, is very much alive, and, on the surface, their vitals seem pretty on point, considering the whole... *stationary* aspect of their current physical state. But my gut feeling—" She swiped lazily at the air between them, already not believing the words she was about to speak. "This is just a passing thing. That said, my team and I will do everything within our capabilities to cure what ails them."

Kim gulped. "Honest—have you ever seen anything like this before? And I'm not talking about something you heard on television or read in a report. I mean, have you personally ever dealt with anything as strange as this?"

Amanda stared at the woman, trying to gauge her intelligence. She seemed smart. Business savvy. A little rough around the edges, which Amanda feared would conflict with her own personality, her way of handling certain social situations. But the woman was definitely smart. A fast learner. Right now, she looked rather manic, on the verge of a major mental collapse. Amanda couldn't blame her, not totally; she had good reason to panic. This sort of thing could ruin a business, especially one that prided itself on being a clean and sick-free residence. As director, she had a lot to lose; her job chief among them.

"No, Mrs. Charon. I have not."

She nodded. "Okay then. Yeah, feel free to do whatever you need to. If you need anything from me or the staff, be sure to let me know."

"I will. And I do. You can start by making a few phone calls."

"Phone calls?"

"Yes. First, I want you to call every available hand you have into work. Overtime is no issue—I'll make sure you're reimbursed every penny. We're going to need all the help we can once the local media gets wind of this. Hell, something as bizarre as this might even attract national attention. Though we can't worry too much about that yet, I'd like to be prepared."

"Dear Christ."

"Yes, well, what did you think would happen?" She waited for an answer that never came.

"Anything else I can do?"

"Yes. You can start calling these people's relatives as well. I want profiles on our seven lucky *guests*. I want a list of every prescription they've ever taken, what they're currently taking, and where they've been in the last seventy-two hours, especially if they've left the premises. Lastly, I want to know who has visited them within that same timeframe. I want to know if those people have left the country in the past two weeks. Can you handle all of that?"

"Absolutely." She seemed insulted that Amanda had subtly suggested otherwise. But Amanda didn't care. She could be insulted all she wanted, as long as she got the job done.

"Good," she said, working her lips into a semblance of a smile. "Then let's get to work."

2

"**D**ROPPED THE SALIVA** samples off at the lab," Barnes said, entering the little makeshift office Amanda had set up in the small conference room to the left of the main lobby. "Should have the results later this afternoon."

"Excellent." She was on the facility's laptop going through the security footage from earlier that morning. Toggling between different camera angles, Amanda stopped and focused on a woman in the corner of the lobby. She was reading a book, a Louis L'Amour paperback, and holding it extremely close to her face. Her glasses, unnecessarily giant, magnified her eyes. At exactly seven a.m., the women jerked her head to the left, as if someone had whispered something into her ear. She appeared confused, pondering a response. Then she went rigid, her back straightening and arching back. Her mouth opened in a scream, as if someone was driving a knife into her stomach, in and out, over and over again, and then her body began to spasm. The paperback tumbled to the floor. The convulsions lasted about sixty seconds. She gripped the armchair for support the entire time, riding out the seizure. Then the woman froze, her face fixed in that eternal pose, that moment of terrible realization, that crippling instant of abject horror.

"Shit," Barnes said, looking over Amanda's shoulder.

She turned in her seat and Barnes stepped back.

"I've watched almost every one of them, the ones that were caught on camera."

"That's some freaky shit."

"You're not kidding. It all happened at exactly the same time. All seven of them went into this weird seizure. Then, they ended up exactly like that." She pointed at the screen with her pen.

"Still thinking brain-eating parasite?"

Amanda shrugged and rotated back to the screen. "I don't know. Impossible to tell without the lab results. I swear..." She zoomed in on the woman's face. That look. The awful way the muscles were posed, the strained cords of her neck so clearly pronounced despite hiding behind the grainy filter of the raw footage. Her jaw appeared to have come unhinged during the *attack* (that was what she called it now), stuck open as if she were at the dentist. "...it's almost like they became possessed. Like something took them over."

"Possessed?" Barnes snorted. "Come on. You can't be serious."

"I'm not saying that's what it is, silly. It's just like... come on, Barnes. You've seen *The Exorcist,* right?"

Barnes rolled his eyes. "Yes, I've seen it. When I was eight. Couldn't sleep for two weeks after."

"Watching this footage reminds me of that movie." She chewed on her nails absentmindedly. She rewound the footage and watched it again, clicking on different angles.

"Well, *you're* gonna have trouble sleeping if you don't turn it off." Barnes took the mouse from her and x'ed out of the browser. "Come on. Let's grab coffee. The lab should have the results soon."

• • •

Amanda added a creamer and three sugar packets to her coffee and blew on it before taking her first sip. It was her sixth cup of the day, and even though she'd promised her doctor she'd cut down on the caffeine, she couldn't help it. She was running on three hours of sleep, plus the video footage had left her head a little rattled, filled with images of the sixty-niners, their terrified looks and wooden postures.

She hadn't smoked a cigarette in ten years, but once she had browsed through all the available film, the craving had hit her like a tsunami. Caffeine and nicotine had always been her go-tos in times of great stress, and since the latter was much more harmful to her long-term existence, she'd opted to quit the cigs instead of giving up the joe.

"Lab results are back," Barnes said, rushing over to the break room's coffee bar. "And you're not gonna believe it."

"What?" she asked, putting down the paper coffee cup. A splash jumped over the rim and ran over the top of her knuckles, burning her. "Ah, shit."

Barnes helped her with a handful of napkins. She took them and patted the spot dry, and then waved her hand in the air, cooling it off.

"Fuck." She ignored the slight burn and grabbed the papers off the counter. Flipping through them, she felt her brow ascend her forehead. "What?"

"I know," Barnes said, leaning against the counter and folding his arms. "Not a single trace of bacteria or foreign antibodies. The levels are normal, and—"

"They're the same." She continued skimming each page, reading over the results, glancing over the numbers. The names atop the pages were different but the numbers below were identical, which didn't seem plausible. It was possible they could read similarly, even share results on a few lines, but that wasn't the case. Each attribute was *exactly the same.* "There must be some mistake," she added, examining the last few results. Everything from the subject's glucose levels to their white cell counts matched, one hundred percent. And, furthermore, they were all impeccably acceptable levels. Not only were their results all *in range*, they were ideal. Each one represented the epitome of healthy. If this were a math quiz, every single patient would have scored a one hundred, plus bonus points.

"It's wild, that's for sure," Barnes said, picking a random sheet from Amanda's hand. "I mean, I expected the cell counts to vary, be off the mark, considering we could be dealing with an infection of sorts—but no, they're spot on. Unbelievable."

Amanda put the results on the table. "Get me someone in the lab, the person who ran the tests. I want a word with them. There has to be some mistake."

"Phelps already went down that road. She said the lab ran them three times because they'd never seen anything like it either."

Amanda retrieved her cell from her pocket and began tapping away at the numbers.

"Who are you calling?"

"Atlanta."

"For what?"

She put the phone to her ear. "Whatever is happening here is going to require a little more than a simple investigation."

"Reinforcements?"

She nodded, then walked to the other end of the room, abandoning that sixth cup of coffee.

3

KIM CHARON SEEMED like a snooty woman, someone Amanda normally wouldn't engage in a public social setting, but today she had no choice in the matter. Anything that happened within the confines of this facility, anything they discovered, any progress made, she'd have to report to Kim, keep her updated throughout the entire investigation. It was the professional thing to do, the right thing to do, and Amanda prided herself on her ability to keep things appropriate even in sticky situations such as this. Though, that hadn't always been the case and she knew it. She'd come a long way, though. Right now, the important thing was keeping her relationship with Kim amicable, especially since she would need favors, things—*important* things—completed, and fast. Especially since she needed help evacuating everyone from Spring Lakes.

"What do you mean *evacuate?*" The woman trembled when she spoke. Clearly someone who wore her emotions on her pantsuit, Kim Charon was exactly the kind of person Amanda Guerrero loved to deal with. Uptight, difficult assholes were her specialty.

"I *mean* exactly what it sounds like. We need everyone to leave the building at once. Workers and anyone who isn't... *frozen* in place."

"You just told me to call people *into* work."

"Now I'm telling you to send them home. The game has changed. I don't want to risk anyone else's health."

25

"Our health is in danger now? So this is what? Some deadly disease?"

Barnes was happy to chime in. "We don't know yet, not exactly."

"Well," the woman said, growing red, "isn't that your job? To know exactly what the hell is happening here? I mean, I can't just kick out one-hundred and fifty of my guests and my entire staff, several of whom I called in on your recommendation. Where am I supposed to put all of them? Send them to the Holiday Inn? And we're not paying our employees to stay home. You must be out of your minds."

Amanda sighed. She understood the woman's frustration, especially since this wouldn't be an easy task, but she didn't need to act like an insolent child either. "Ma'am, we have options. I suggest you start calling their relatives to see if they wouldn't mind taking in their loved ones until we figure out this thing. If not, we have three local hospitals, all within a reasonable driving distance. Now, my people have already made a few phone calls to St. Augustine and St. Clara and both are willing and able and are expecting to take some extra traffic this afternoon. As far as paying your staff, that's just business. I'll make sure you're reimbursed for the extra help I told you to call in, and I'm sure your insurance company will be happy to assist you with any other financial damages this situation might cause." The woman scoffed at that. "So, as I said—you might want to start making some phone calls, seeing what you can do to alleviate their discomfort and confusion. Because, right now, I bet all one-hundred and forty-three of your *guests* are probably very frightened. And honestly, this isn't the best place for them anyway, not with everything going on."

"This is unacceptable. People are paying for their loved ones to be here. Under our care. They expect a problem-free environment."

"I'll repeat, you can file a claim through your insurance company for any financial setbacks you might incur. We also have access to some government funds for situations like this, which I'd be more than happy to help you file for, so no worries there. But what I *would* worry about is your clients. Your *guests,* as you call them—because... aren't they the most important thing?"

The red woman didn't have a response for that. If she did, she didn't share. Instead, she pulled on the bottom of her suit jacket, raised her chin, and said, "Fine. I'll get working at once."

"I appreciate your cooperation," Amanda told her, a faux smile accompanying the words.

After the woman disappeared around the corner, with her lawyers in tow, Amanda turned back to Barnes. "That went a lot better than expected."

"Thought you were going to lose your cool."

"Almost did."

"Would have liked to see it."

"I bet."

"Phelps and I had a wager."

"Oh?"

"Lunch."

"What side were you on?"

Barnes laughed, ran his hand through his hair. "Not sure if I should tell you."

"If you're worried about my feelings, don't be."

"Okay, I had you blowing up. At least cursing her out, telling her to fuck her own face-hole."

"Come on, man. I'm a little more professional than that."

Her track record didn't exactly support that theory. Last year, while investigating a peculiar flu strain at an elementary school in Buffalo, she had gotten into an altercation with the principal. The two ended up shouting in each other's faces, nose-to-nose, and

27

Amanda had put a hand on her. On her chest. Pushed her a few steps back. That was as far as it had gone, but, if Barnes hadn't been there to drag her away, who knew what would have happened.

You were gonna slug her, Barnes had said.

No, she'd said stubbornly, despite knowing it wasn't far from the truth. There had been a part of her that knew she was capable—more than capable—and, if the scuffle had gone on just a little bit longer, well, hell, she might have decked the intolerable woman.

"Well, maybe just a little more professional than that," she said, having a laugh about it even though it was hardly funny. She could have been fired for laying a hand on the woman, and again, Barnes had gone to bat for her, smoothed things over with the school's administrators, convinced them not to report the incident.

"I was thinking we were in Buffalo all over again."

"Hm. Buffalo. My favorite place." She jabbed his arm. "Come on, Barnes. Give me an ounce of credit. I've behaved myself lately."

"Okay, okay. Just an ounce. Nothing more."

Silence claimed the next fifteen seconds.

Barnes scanned the empty conference room. "So... what's next?"

"Well," Amanda said, picking up the paperwork, shuffling through it and glancing over the identical numbers the lab had reported, hoping to discover something she had missed. But there was nothing except the same results printed over and over again. The names changed, but the blood work stayed the same down to the smallest fraction.

She considered their options. "Let's monitor their vitals while we wait for direction from Atlanta." Blood work and saliva samples were all they could really do right now, unless they cracked one of the sixty-niners' heads open and took a tissue sample of their brain—but they were nowhere near that stage yet, nor would they be unless one of them died. And, so far, every single one of the infected was still alive, even if their appearance suggested otherwise. Science proved them to be alive. All seven of them. Healthy as could be. Dead on the outside. Alive within.

"Okay," Barnes said, then squinted as if fighting off the onset of a killer headache. "Hey, did Kim tell you one of the guards tried to move one of them?"

She looked up from the papers. "No? Why would he do that?"

"Said he wanted to lay her on a bed or something. I don't know all the details, but he went for it. And you know what?"

She waited.

"Guy said the elderly woman didn't budge. He couldn't move her. And I quote, 'Sir, I weigh two-seventy and played defensive tackle in college. I could move a wall if I needed to. That woman didn't budge from her seat, not a millimeter.' She couldn't have weighed more than a hundred pounds."

"Interesting."

"More than interesting. Impossible. He said it was like she'd been filled with concrete."

Amanda recalled how hard the man with the cane had felt to the touch. He'd felt solid, and so cold, cold and hard like a block of ice. His flesh had not rebelled against her touch and, as weird as she had thought that was at the time, it was even stranger after hearing the guard's experience.

What the hell is happening here?

"I have to admit, Amanda," Barnes said, all traces of his humor erased, "I don't like the vibes I'm getting from this place."

"Oh Christ. Not this again."

"I'm serious this time."

"You and your vibes."

"You don't think it's weird?"

"Of course, I think it's weird. But there's a rational, scientific explanation for all of this, and we'll dig to the bottom of it. Don't worry. We always do."

"Okay. Fine. Whatever you say. I'm just saying, you were the one who brought up *The Exorcist* earlier."

She twisted her lips. "That's just what the footage reminded me of. Never claimed these people were possessed by Pazuzu."

"Yeah, you're right. I don't believe in that shit anyway. However... if this *does* turn out to be some kind of demonic possession case, you owe me a beer. Or twelve."

"Joe, we both know you don't drink. Not anymore."

He pinched her cheek. "Ten years sober tomorrow, actually."

"Congrats, kid."

"Oh, I'm a kid now, am I? Thought I was at least six years older than you."

"Yeah, but I'm your boss. So, it's like you're my kid."

"Not sure how to take that, honestly."

She slapped his shoulder with the file. "Take it however you want. We got work to do. Let's split up. I want you to record pulses, heart rates, and noticeable changes in complexion or..." She almost said behavior, but that was dumb because there *was no* behavior. These people were statues. Dead to the world, though, not really. "...or, any noticeable differences from before."

The door to the conference room swung inward, and Kim Charon appeared with her squad drifting in behind her. She seemed out of breath and hunched over once she crossed the threshold. The two lawyers had their hands on her back and kept whispering "Are you okay, Kim?" into her ear, over and over again, until she told them how fine she was.

"What's the matter?" Amanda asked, pangs of nervous panic hammering away at her chest.

Kim stood up, catching her breath. "One of them... *one of them moved.*"

4

S SOON AS she stepped inside Manuel Renteria's dorm, Amanda smelled the sticky-sweet scent of pipe-smoke and cheap cologne, and was instantly transported back to another time, another place. That time was twenty-seven years ago when she was six years old, and that place was her grandfather's home just outside of El Paso, Texas, about five miles from the Mexican border. The odor alone almost caused her to exit the room prematurely, but once she saw the face of the frozen man, got a good glimpse at the mustache clinging to his upper lip, she literally leaped back over the threshold and into the hallway. An inward cry escaped her mouth. She bumped into the wall, and Barnes rushed over to her side, his eyes enlarged, his forehead creased with concern.

"What the hell, Amanda?" he asked her quietly, not making a big production out of it. "Are you okay?"

Neither Kim nor her lawyers paid much attention to her reaction. They were filing into the room, their eyes glued on the stiff in the corner. Manuel's eyes were bulging, staring into some foreign world beyond this one, his mouth stretched wide as if he'd meant to fill it with a hoagie. Once everyone had made their initial observation, they turned to Amanda, waiting for her to finally enter the room and give the old man a quick visual examination, for whatever that was worth.

Not much, she thought, bouncing off the wall. "I'm fine," she told Barnes in a whisper, and then crossed the threshold, entered the room, and walked over to her newest patient.

The man in question, Manuel Renteria, looked oddly like her grandfather. The eerie resemblance had knocked her off balance, both mentally and physically. A cluster of memories had come rushing back to her, none of them inspiring. A cold sweat had broken out beneath her hairline. Her nerves stirred, causing her bones to rattle, and tingle with the onset of fear-induced numbness. She heard her teeth chattering and wondered if anyone else in the room heard it too. She wasn't prepared to answer the questions they were sure to ask if they caught her behaving this way.

The closer she got to the old man, the more dread set in, perching on her flesh, digging in like a hawk's talons.

Her mouth dried up. Words were hard to come by, and, although she knew the moment would pass and everything would be fine, that this weird bout of *deja vu* and the punch of memories that had kissed her brain would soon end, the thought of opening her mouth and articulating language made her want to puke.

"Are you okay, Mrs. Guerero?" Kim asked, eyeing her suspiciously. Even the lawyers were inspecting her, noticing every new bead of sweat that dotted the skin above her eyebrows. "You look... sick."

She shook her head, letting the whole *Mrs.* thing slide. She was in no mood to correct the woman. "No, I'm fine," she said, and miraculously the words came out sounding normal, her voice showing no inconsistencies. "Haven't eaten yet. Just hungry." She swallowed. "Now, you say the old man *moved?*"

"That's what one of the nurses said when she came in here to check on him. Carmel. Said the man's eyes moved and so did his jaw."

"Barnes," Amanda said, turning to her subordinate, though she never thought of him as such. Only in jest. Otherwise, she treated him as her equal, much to the chagrin of *her* management team. "See if you can track down Nurse Carmel. Interview her. I want explicit details of what she saw. Document everything. Have her write a statement."

"Yes, boss." He left the room at once.

She hated when he called her boss, even if it was their little joke.

Taking her flashlight and directing it at the old man's face, she tensed, expecting him to blink, expecting his leg to twitch, expecting his arm to shoot out and grab hold of her throat. None of those things happened as she shone the light in his eyes, letting the glow linger there for a solid twenty seconds. His pupils shriveled just like they had on the other patients. There was a coldness to the man's eyes, and she wondered if that was because they resembled her grandfather's so... so uncannily.

Her grandfather.

(go ahead, pequeña, touch it.)

She shivered, a trail of cold fingers tapping along her spine. Spending a second in her childhood was enough to induce vomiting, despite there being nothing in her stomach to expunge. Shaking away those memories, she continued to examine Manuel's condition.

"What do you think?" Kim asked.

Amanda clicked off the flashlight. "He looks the same as the others. Nothing different about him. Nothing I can tell anyway."

"Do you think Carmel is making it up?"

Amanda shrugged. "I mean, why would she? Is she the kind of person who'd lie about something like this?"

Kim shook her head without hesitation. "She's one of the best staff members we have."

"Then... I dunno. Maybe it was a reflex or something. Some kind of involuntary reaction. These people are alive, as far as I can tell. There seems to be something happening up here, in their brains. They're reacting to light. Blood is pumping. Neurons are firing. Just guessing, but I'm pretty sure they've become prisoners inside their own bodies. Whatever it is, this parasite, it's attacking the cerebellum, the part of the brain that controls movement. That said, a muscle will move and twitch—and that's normal. Happens to everyone on a daily basis—a muscle spasm here and there, though, because we're so active and concentrating on other things, we hardly notice it."

Kim tucked her hands in her pockets, shifting uncomfortably, as if her blue suit suddenly constricted around her body. Amanda understood the woman's on-edge reaction to everything that was happening. It couldn't have been easy for her, this situation. After all, as the director, she was responsible for everything that happened at Spring Lakes, and had the final say about how certain situations were handled.

"I can have my assistant, Phelps, hook Mr. Renteria up to a brain monitor. I was going to start monitoring the patients in the common area, but we can start with Mr. Renteria here, in light of his... positive response. We'll use his results as a baseline when we examine the others."

Kim nodded in agreement. The lawyers did not protest, even though they looked like they wanted to rebuke everything. Amanda noticed that Hatterman's demeanor had changed, slightly. He almost looked as terrified as Kim, scared of what the brain monitor might reveal. For some reason, Amanda got the sense that Hatterman and Hart were already in defense mode, strategizing how they could spin the results so that none of the fault fell back on Spring Lakes. She also sensed that Kim cared less about her guests' wellbeing than she did about the potential hit to the facility's pocketbook, if they were to be found at fault and later sued by the guests' loved ones.

Above all, the three of them were scared shitless. Amanda recognized the fear, as it was practically printed on their foreheads.

Amanda was frightened too, though it had nothing to do with the patients and what was happening to them—her focus was currently on Mr. Renteria, *Manuel,* and the physical traits he shared with her long-dead (good riddance) *abuelo.* She did not show fear; inside, her stomach melted away, her bones felt like they'd liquified. Her limbs felt as if they were made of rubber, pliable extensions of her numb framework. A bitter taste claimed her mouth, an acidic hint of bile. She'd never experienced a panic attack before—had friends who claimed to have them regularly and took medication for it—but now, in Mr. Renteria's dorm, she assumed she was experiencing one.

A full-blown panic attack.

Her lungs felt nonexistent.

She slipped the mask away from her mouth, letting it hang around her neck.

A sharp, quick intake of air came from Kim's direction. Behind her mask, Amanda pictured her lips forming a giant zero.

"I just... need some air," Amanda explained, heading for the door.

"Aren't you afraid you'll catch it, too!" Kim half-asked, half-yelled to her.

Amanda didn't have time to explain how parasites worked, how they couldn't enter her body like an air particle. Besides, she wasn't wholly convinced of that theory. The range of possibilities were endless, and, for some unknown reason, she still hadn't abandoned her *Exorcist* hunch.

As she made her way down the hall, toward the exit, she did feel something crawling around her insides, and she doubted the sickly feeling had anything to do with the minor panic attack.

No, this was something else.

Something bad.

And it was happening to her, *here,* in this place.

As she pushed through the exit and felt the warmth of the afternoon on her flesh, the fresh air zoom up her nostrils and inflate her lungs, the awfulness of what lived inside Spring Lakes bled away, as did the memories of the man who'd always haunt her.

5

LINDA PHELPS FINISHED wrapping Manuel Renteria's head with what looked like a giant hairnet, only this hairnet contained dozens of tiny electrodes. Once the headpiece was secure, Phelps sat in front of her mobile computer monitor. She hesitated to flip on the switch, and instead turned to Barnes.

"Shouldn't Amanda be here for this?" she asked, wincing as if the question had caused her pain. She pushed her glasses back up her nose and waited for Barnes to reply.

"Amanda had to step out for a minute," he told the room consisting of Phelps, Kim, and the lawyers. The nurses had been instructed to keep the non-infected comfortable until their loved ones came to pick them up, or until the buses showed to take them to the nearest medical facility. "She'll be right back. In the meantime, she's given us the go ahead."

Phelps faced the computer and did as Barnes told her. Flicking the switch from off to on, her heart skipped like a flat stone across a still pond. She didn't know why, not exactly. Their current situation was peculiar, sure, something she'd never come across in her ten years of further education, or on the other lone case she'd been sent to investigate to start her young career. Yes, she'd seen infectious diseases that rendered their victims stiff, incapacitated, on the verge of almost certain death, but those diseases usually carried physical symptoms—

lesions, decay, bouts of vomiting, jaundice. The guests of Spring Lakes exhibited none of those visible ailments, and, other than being frozen stiff and impossible to move, their bodies figuratively turning to stone—there was nothing abnormal about them, at least nothing evident given what the blood work and saliva samples stated. She'd seen the paperwork herself. Every single line was in range, down to the most trivial vitamin level. And not just in range, no. *Perfect.* Right on target. An archetype example of what a person should be. A flawless score.

This, above the other symptoms, kept her on edge, prodded her nerves.

This was only her second field case and it was already beginning to prove to be a problematic assignment. She wanted to be back home in her Atlanta apartment, curled up on her couch with Mr. Perkins, her one-year-old labradoodle, reading a book, probably the newest Karin Slaughter release. None of what had happened at Spring Lakes—what was continuing to happen—felt *right*. The feeling of impending doom snuck up on her, as if the bottom of the world was threatening to fall out from under them, like this facility and the grounds it had been built upon were about to slide into a massive sinkhole and disappear into the earth's endless dark chasm, never to be seen or heard from again.

She shook her head, washing away the dismal thoughts that plagued her.

"Phelps?" Barnes said, clearing his throat. When she didn't respond right away, he placed a comforting hand on her shoulder.

She realized she hadn't flipped the switch after all. Her finger was still pressed on it, trembling. Every eye in the room latched onto her, and she instantly grew hot with embarrassment.

"Would you... do you... need help?" Barnes offered her a smile. The others weren't smiling; they wore long faces, failing to shield their discontent. She could tell they didn't approve of Amanda's methods, that, if it were up to them, this whole operation would shut down faster than Kim could snap her fingers.

But despite their looks of general disapproval, she could tell they were scared. Phelps knew they weren't, but for some reason, it felt like they were hiding something. Maybe that was her projecting, the freaky situation to blame for her wandering thoughts and absent-minded approach to the task at hand.

Freaky.

This whole thing is beyond freaky, she thought, and a walked-through-cobwebs feeling coated her neck and arms, trickled down her back.

"No," she finally said. "I'm fine." But she wasn't, and she didn't know why.

She flipped the switch. The screen lit up before her, alive with the map of the old man's brain. Each electrode pulsed on screen, burning with information. And that information told her everything inside Mr. Renteria's noggin was A-okay. There was no damage to any of the regions, especially to the man's cerebellum, the part of the brain Amanda had been most concerned about.

Barnes pointed to the screen. The others leaned over, especially the two lawyers. Phelps felt their breath and the scent of their aftershave come crawling up her nose. It was a sour, almost ancient smell, one that reminded her of the barbershop her father used to take her to. From the corner of her eye, she saw one of them—Hatterman, she thought—peeking over her shoulder. He looked the same as his partner, only taller. They both wore the same glasses and, if Phelps had to wager, she'd bet the men were related somehow. Brothers or first cousins. Related for sure. Hatterman inspected the screen with such intensity that Phelps swore he knew what he was looking at.

"What are we looking at?" Hatterman asked. A bead of sweat appeared near his temple and dribbled down his cheek.

Barnes put his hand up and moved the man back a foot. "Some very expensive equipment. Prefer if you wouldn't breathe on it."

The lawyer didn't take too kindly to that and looked like he wanted to protest his removal. In the end, he kept his mouth shut. A glance from the shorter lawyer might have factored into that decision. Hart was the quieter of the two, and, judging from their brief interaction, the smarter of the two.

"See this," Barnes told them, pointing to the bright spots on the electronic 3-D rendered image of Renteria's brain. "This is what we're monitoring. These are integral portions of the brain used in all basic human function. We're simply monitoring to see if they're sending and receiving messages from other parts of the brain."

The lights took turns growing bright, then dimming. They glowed like fireflies on a summer night, coming and going naturally. Constantly changing. Constantly working. Constantly firing their ammunition off to each other, sharing responses and vital information, necessary tasks for basic cerebral function.

There was nothing abnormal about the brain map. On the surface, Renteria's head seemed to be working the way it should.

Another act that unnerved Phelps.

What is wrong with them? she asked herself. *What the hell is going on with these people?*

And furthermore, what was the significance of sixty-nine? It was the question she'd first asked herself when she'd heard the report, before Amanda Guerrero had asked her to come along. It seemed like an odd number. Why weren't sixty-eight-year-olds afflicted? Sixty-eight-and-a-half? Seventy? Phelps had overheard Kim talking to one of the lawyers earlier, telling him that a Patricia Devlin was six days shy of her sixty-ninth birthday, yet, she had awoken that morning feeling fine and frosty, the same as she had the day before. Even better. Her mood—not ordinarily chipper and often quite forgetful—was upbeat and positive, didn't even complain about how fluffy the pancakes were during breakfast. She had remembered everything that had happened the day before. Her nurses said it was the best behavior Patricia Devlin had exhibited in the last six months. She'd even remembered things that had happened eight months ago, and, as someone who was stricken with pre-Alzheimer's dementia, that was *really* good. She didn't drift or wander, as the residents of Spring Lakes were occasionally apt to. No, she was lucid, intelligent, and a real pleasure to be around.

More evidence to throw on the *weirdness* pile.

A chill cascaded down Phelps's back, causing her entire body to shake uncontrollably. A quick twitch, barely noticeable. No one in the room seemed to catch it, and, if they had, they didn't mention it.

Maybe because they feel it too. The chill. It's in the air, clinging to us.

Whatever was happening here was palpable. She felt it in every breath. Every moment. Every word spoken seemed to be coated with the disease, the thing that had come to take over Spring Lakes.

The thing.

What was it? She kept asking herself that, and still, her thoughts came up empty. She had nothing. Except for a map of Manuel Renteria's brain and all that showed was that the man's head was fine. Healthy. Firing on all cylinders.

"So..." Kim Charon said, breaking the stretch of silence. It had gone on far too long, and even though she didn't care for the woman and her arrogance, Phelps was glad she had opened her mouth. "What the hell has happened to him?" Then she corrected herself: *"Them."*

"According to this," Barnes said, motioning to the EEG machine, "everything looks fine."

"What do you mean it looks fine?"

"It means..." said another voice, entering the room. It belonged to Amanda. She looked pale, as if she'd spent her entire break throwing up the sandwich she'd eaten during the flight. Even her lips looked gray, like a pair of dead worms that rested on the lower half of her face. "...it means that this man's brain is fully functioning."

"So... they're not sick?" Kim asked, sounding lost. In the woman's defense, none of this was making sense to her either.

"No, they're sick. Just whatever it is isn't limiting their brain function. Which reduces the possibility of it being some brain-eating bacteria or MRSA."

"So, what does that mean for our guests?" Kim sounded more panicked than ever. Like she was about to start screaming, demanding answers, threatening people if results weren't soon delivered. The pitch of her voice had climbed with each word. "I mean, you're supposed to be figuring this out, aren't you? That's why you've come?"

"We're trying," Amanda said. Phelps got the sense she wanted to add the word *bitch* onto the end of her statement. That she showed some restraint actually impressed her, especially given Dr. Guerrero's well-documented and much-talked-about history of losing her temper. Whether it was true she had punched a colleague in the face during her first year at the CDC over a heated conversation about that year's particular influenza strain or just hearsay, she didn't know. Phelps suspected she wouldn't still have a job if that was the case, but who knew. The rumor remained unconfirmed, and Phelps was much too shy to ask the woman herself.

"Well, try harder." Kim flashed her pearly whites. "You've been here for two hours already and we have no more answers than when you waltzed in here so confidently. The only thing you've told me is how to run my business."

Now it was Amanda who bared her teeth. "I evacuated those who weren't infected for the public safety of the other guests, and your employees. That's standard operating procedure, Mrs. Charon."

"And what have you done about our safety?" With her finger, she gestured to those in the room.

"No one is making you stay. You're free to leave with the others; in fact, I recommend it." Her sardonic smile formed naturally.

"I bet you'd like that, Mrs. Guerrero, I really do. But if you think for a second that I'm leaving you alone here, with my guests, making decisions about their well-being without me and my legal team's consent... then you have another thing coming."

"I think it would be better if you let us do our jobs. Interference will only add risk. Plus, as your legal team is already aware, I can file an emergency judgment. We have our own legal representatives in the area and their turnaround is super quick in emergency cases, such as this."

Kim looked to her legal team. Hatterman and Hart only raised their bushy eyebrows.

Phelps tensed. Lowered her head. She wasn't a big fan of confrontation and tried to avoid these situations at all costs.

"I think it would be better if you did *your* jobs," the director said venomously, as she turned back toward the rest of the room.

Phelps watched Amanda's cheeks blossom with anger. She stepped in front of her boss, before she could open her mouth, and spoke for her. "Mrs. Charon. Please. There's no need to behave this way. I assure you we're doing everything we can—"

"Everything you can?" The woman huffed, folded her arms. "I don't think—"

It was Barnes's turn to chime in. "Look," he said, putting up his hands, facing a palm to each side of the room. "Arguing about this is pointless and counterproductive. We're going to figure this thing out. More CDC officials are on their way up from Atlanta." He checked his watch. "They're flying into a private airport in a couple hours. We'll continue to monitor vitals and issue blood work and saliva samples every hour to make sure nothing changes. You," he said to Kim, "do your best to keep the other guests safe and comfortable until their transportation arrives. That's your job right now."

The woman looked as if she wanted to protest some more, then—wisely—thought better of it.

"In the meantime," Barnes said, turning to the computer where Phelps had sat back down. "Open up Matrix X," he told her.

"Matrix X?" Kim asked, sounding concerned. "What is that?"

"It's a computer program," Phelps said, surprised by the sound of her own voice. She was usually quiet when things were tense, but she felt like she needed to take some of the heat off her co-workers. Focus the attention on herself for a moment, even though the spotlight, having all the eyes on her, was probably her least favorite thing in the world. "It allows us to interact with and stimulate brainwaves by using the scanner helmet."

"Interact?" She demanded clarification, and Phelps wasn't sure how to elaborate on the intricacies of the program without blowing the woman's mind.

"Yes," said Barnes, gnawing on the round end of his pen. "We can send little electrical impulses to each one of the electrodes, give them a little poke. To see how they respond to stimulation."

Hart raised a finger and opened his mouth. "And what will that accomplish precisely?"

Seeming to have cooled off, Amanda was the first to respond. "We can see if the brain will respond or if it's damaged in any way. I mean, on the surface everything looks good. These are healthy signals coming from Mr.... uh..."

"Renteria," Kim said. Her eyebrows remained bent, and Phelps wondered if they were permanently fixed that way.

"Yes. Mr. Renteria, of course." She cleared her throat. Something about the man, his name, had caught Amanda by surprise, but Phelps hadn't thought much of it. "Mr. Renteria's brain looks very healthy, especially in his current state of—for the lack of a more medically accurate term—temporary rigor mortis."

Kim Charon seemed satisfied by this answer, and so did her weaselly-looking lawyers. The creases in their foreheads smoothed out over the next few minutes, while Barnes went on to explain the program with a little more detail, throwing in some technical jargon just to confuse them. Phelps got a small kick out of it, despite the growing sensation in the pit of her stomach. No one asked another question about Matrix X, and the director and her two lawyers didn't object to further testing.

The lingering uneasiness prowled Phelps's nerves, her mind. There was a sense that something bad was waiting for them up ahead, along the path. She wanted to purge those feelings, those harrowing thoughts, trim the sense of impending doom from her mind.

But she didn't know how.

Instead, she opened Matrix X and got to work.

6

AMANDA REALLY WISHED Kim and her lawyers had left the room to attend to the needs of the others, *had actually fucking listened to her instructions,* but the trio hung around, stalking their every move. If she didn't know any better, she'd guess they knew something about what had happened here and didn't want the truth uncovered. They watched over them like a teenager would their parents going through their underwear drawer, knowing damn well they'd discover a secret stash of dirty magazines and marijuana paraphernalia.

She locked those thoughts away and looked over Phelps's shoulder, directing her finger at the screen. "Try this one."

Phelps clicked away. On screen, a small dot lit up orange, which meant the cluster of electrodes in that region gave off a tiny electrical impulse, stimulating an entire quadrant of Renteria's brain.

"Let's see how Mr. Renteria's sensory strip responds," Amanda announced to the room, feeling the need to narrate every step.

They waited thirty seconds. Then, the little on-screen dot that had been orange turned green, letting them know the brain had received the input and had responded accordingly. Normal. This was the expected result from an ordinary, properly functioning brain.

"Okay." Amanda stood up straight. "Success."

"He's okay then?" Kim took a break from chewing on her fingernails to pose the question.

"The sensory strip is aware of exterior input. A little slow to react, but that's fine."

"Slow?"

"Took about thirty seconds to respond. But we have brain activity, a fair amount of it, so that's a win." Amanda pointed to another spot on the monitor. "Let's test the cerebellum."

Phelps did as she was instructed, clicking on the back portion of the brain. Tiny lights buzzed with an orange glow, brightening the screen.

They waited.

Longer this time.

Amanda checked her watch. *Forty-five seconds. Fifty. Fifty-five.* She glanced around nervously, surveying the others. Barnes paced in the background, near the man's closet. Kim continued to gnaw away on her fingernails. The lawyers looked on, beads of sweat forming on what could pass as a hairline. She could feel their collective stares penetrating her, attempting to steal her thoughts. As if they thought she was hiding something.

A minute twenty. A minute thirty.

No response.

"I don't understand," Kim said. "The other responded just fine. What's wrong with his cere-bella?"

"Cerebell*um*," she corrected. "And just because it's not responding to our input, doesn't mean—"

The screen lit up, the entire cluster of electrodes reporting a vibrant green signal.

"There." She was about to comment on their success when the rest of the screen brightened with dots, all of them green and glowing. The entire map brightened like a string of Christmas lights. Every single electrode pulsed with life, going from bright to brighter, then back to bright again. Over and over, the sensors repeated the process, filling the map with activity that Amanda had never seen before. They were all responding, even though Phelps hadn't touched a thing.

"I didn't do it," Phelps said, rolling her chair away from the computer.

"What is it?" Kim squawked.

Amanda leaned in, her brow bending. "Not sure..."

On screen, the seconds between the firefly-like pulsing shortened. In no time at all they were flashing like strobe lights in a nightclub, all of them in sync, feeding off each other's pace. The collection of bright lights gave Amanda an instant headache, forcing her eyes shut.

"What is it?" the intolerable woman asked again, the anger in her voice no longer concealed. Her vocal pitch hit Amanda's ears like some unpleasant, discordant clatter. "I demand to know—"

Amanda drowned out whatever came next. The lights had carried her away into a trance. All the blinking, the persistent glow of the lively electrodes had stolen her away from the room. Her concentration had led her to the flickering orbs, dozens of them. It was as if they had spoken to her. Whispers filled her ears. Voices somewhere in the distance. Perhaps miles away. Perhaps... *farther.* Perhaps everywhere around her, all at once. In her head. A cacophony of songs, a choir of unseen members filling the silence she had created, seeking solace.

Not whispers. Not voices. Not songs.

One voice. A single mouth moving in the dark.

(touch it)

Familiar voices now. Sound. She could smell the past, permeating the air around her, the darkness her mind currently inhabited. Faint, but present.

(present, the voice says, it's a present, open it up)

The monitor disappeared. The whole room faded into a long black hallway. Everything around her wore dark shadows, everything except the old man sitting in the chair.

He wasn't paralyzed anymore.

(open it, zip-zip)

(touch it)

(tickle it)

His gaze was on her, though his eyes were different. Gone. Replaced by something cloudy, a white murky glaze. Something swirled within them, dark, as if someone had injected ink into his eyeballs. The dark tendrils twisted and coiled, moving about in serpentine patterns, tainting the pure white as it roamed. Before long, everything inside the man's eyes was black. Soulless. Obsidian oceans. Movement beneath. Things swam there. Terrible things.

(it's just a game)

(go ahead)

Mr. Renteria was smiling. Though it wasn't Renteria. Not anymore. Amanda didn't know what it was, but, whatever the man had become, it surely wasn't human.

It's his smile, she thought, watching the ends of his lips curl in a way that hardened her flesh, caused bumps to ripple down the length of her arms. The hairs on her neck became erect, sending chills from her shoulders to her lower half, so low even her toes caught the bitter sensation.

Yes, it was his smile. But something else, too. The way his arms looked, how they appeared longer than they should. They hung lower, the end of his fingertips ending somewhere around his ankles. His head was angled crookedly, like it had been broken at some point in his life and never healed correctly. Or at all. His cranium was malformed as well, dented in odd places. He was a hideous sight, and, for the life of her, she couldn't remember if he'd looked that way twenty seconds ago, before the room had cozied with the shadows.

Before his eyes had gone black.

Amanda wanted to speak, but her voice failed her.

"*Go ahead,*" Renteria said, though the voice did not belong to him. "*Touch it. I won't tell. Neither will you. It'll be our little secret.*"

She wanted to cry as she had on the day her grandfather had spoken those same exact words in that same *exact* voice. Not the same tone or inflection, but *that same damn voice.*

She choked out a word, assumed it was "No" because that was what she wanted to say.

"*It's okay,*" he promised, just as he had long ago.

She was somewhere else now. The shadows had given away to an enclosed porch. Outside the screen walls lay an endless desert. Not how she remembered it, but close enough. Whenever she dreamed of this place, there were houses bordering her grandfather's property, houses with neighbors, just like there had been in real life. But there might as well have been nothing back there, nothing but an infinite stretch of dirt and sand and clay earth, because no one had come to her rescue then, and no one would come to her rescue now.

Her grandfather stood, locked the door. She wondered where her parents were. The store? A movie? Out to dinner? She wondered if they cared. *Fuck,* if they *knew.* She'd never know. Not even when she'd broken her promise.

(*tell no one*)

(*our secret*)

That smile on his lips, that sick curvature shaping the lower half of his face. The way his lips pushed his mustache around made it come alive like some fuzzy, gray caterpillar. Dark lines appeared on his cheeks, drawing shadows across his skin. They matched the darkness that fell around her.

She hated him then, hated him now.

Then came the finger, the one he placed over his lips. Next his hands went to his belt. After he loosened the buckle and slipped the leather through the metal loop, he grabbed his zipper. Pulled down. Freed himself. He cupped his genitals, held them like a small kitten. Like something gentle. Something pure and innocent, not to be harmed. Mishandled. Next, he let them go, releasing them like a bird to the wind.

(touch it)

The lights went out.

Darkness all around them.

Amanda felt herself shrink back into reality.

"What the hell just happened?" she heard Kim ask, and, as much as her voice eroded her patience, she was glad to have heard it. Because there were certainly worse voices out there, speaking in the dark. Whispering. Waiting.

(touch it, taste it)

Sick panic stirred within her.

A second later the emergency lights kicked on, washing the room in frail light, which seemed bright compared to the impenetrable dark from moments ago. Renteria now stood before them, his head angled back, gazing up at the ceiling as if a bright, endless starscape hovered above them, revealing a beautiful scene that no one could resist.

But Amanda saw nothing but painted plaster that was peeling in the corners.

"Mr. Renteria?" Kim called to him. "Mr. Renteria, can you hear me?"

Amanda shushed her. Kim scowled, a series of spasms afflicting her upper lip.

Renteria continued to hold the ceiling in high regard. Barnes stepped away from his position behind the computer and walked over to him, cautiously, as if the man could spring forth at any second, seize him by the neck and wring him dead.

After examining the still frozen man, Barnes directed the flashlight at his eyes. "The same," he said, squinting, examining the pupils, on the lookout for any changes.

Amanda, her face strained with discontent, sidled up next to him. She gave Renteria her own once over, also failing to recognize any changes, other than the obvious—the man was standing now instead of sitting. *He had moved. He had stood right up.*

He'd done so in the dark, and that got her mind working in several directions, scattering her thoughts like a handful of marbles hitting the hardwood floor. After she had compiled the information at hand, compartmentalized and broken down everything, what she'd witnessed and tested, she had come to the stunning realization that they knew no more about the mysterious disease than when they'd arrived. None of it made any sense. The strange paralysis, the unusual brain functions. None of the symptoms the patients had exhibited lined up with anything she'd seen before, or had even *heard of.* This was new territory, whatever it was, and Amanda was certain she didn't want any part of whatever this disease (if that's what it was) offered.

And then there was the vision.

Yes, don't forget about that.

It had felt so real. Like she'd literally been transported into the past, twenty-seven years ago, and she could still smell the cigarillo smoke that had been baked into the furniture on her grandfather's porch. The scent sickened her, churned whatever was left in her stomach. She felt dirty. Filthy. Like something contaminated her, a greasy membrane that no soap could absolve. She felt...

...broken.

Among other things, she felt broken. Like a piece of her was missing. No, not missing.

Stolen.

He took something from me.

Yes. He had. A piece that would continue to stay missing, something she could never get back. It was lost, that piece of her. Hidden, and never to be found. Gone forever.

"Amanda," Barnes said, snapping her out of another haunted stupor. "Look at this."

He angled the flashlight so the beam of light shot down Renteria's throat. His mouth was center stage in the dim room. She stood on her toes and peeked inside, waiting for Barnes to point out what he'd seen in—what appeared to be—the mouth an ordinary old man. Silver fillings sparkled under the tunnel of bright light.

"What is it?" she asked, sharpening her vision, trying to lock onto whatever it was Barnes intended to show her.

"There." He nodded as if that somehow clarified the mystery object's position.

She looked into the hollow of Renteria's throat, and, in the back, tucked off to the right, sandwiched between a fold of muscle and the man's tonsil, was something white.

"Tonsil stone?" she asked. The small object, no bigger than a shriveled pea, was mostly white but also yellow. The man's breath was atrocious, and she figured if they were to dig around long enough, they'd discover more pressing issues than tonsil stones.

"Don't know. Maybe. Looks... bigger." With his free hand, he snapped his fingers. "I need tweezers. Now. Phelps or anyone."

Phelps hopped off her seat without hesitation and darted toward the door. It was almost as if she wanted a reprieve from the situation, or more specifically—away from Kim Charon and her two lackeys. As if the room had held her prisoner and Barnes's request was the key that unlocked her restraints. Maybe she'd seen something in the darkness too, Amanda thought.

Maybe they all had.

Phelps returned in record time. She handed Barnes the tweezers, and Barnes inserted the metal instrument into the old man's mouth. Amanda caught Kim opening her *own* mouth, perhaps to protest, perhaps to object to the intrusion, but her jaw closed under the advisement of no one. Amanda wanted to tell the woman to keep her fucking mask on but decided against it. She'd warned them enough. Whatever they did was now at their own risk.

Barnes locked onto the small object, and it moved very unlike a tonsil stone. It was more delicate than a packed nugget of solid bacteria. It moved like...

Paper?

It did. Like wet newspaper, only it didn't break apart and held together through the entire extraction. After he had removed the small piece of paper, Barnes let it dangle before everyone in the room, let it hang there as proof, proof that what they'd seen was real.

Amanda took her gloved hand and held it out, breathing heavily into the paper dome that covered her mouth. Barnes dropped the paper, about the size of a fortune cookie ribbon, on her palm.

She immediately flattened it out with her other finger and silently read the words printed there.

Her heart skidded, stopped, and began beating again, only more furiously this go around. Shivers fell upon her like rainfall, pounding all parts of her body at once.

"What is it?" Barnes asked. "What does it say?"

She made a fist around the paper, sealing its message from the others, and then dropped it on the floor.

Amanda stormed out of the room, ignoring the barrage of inquiries. Not because she didn't want to answer their questions—she didn't, true, but that wasn't why. It was because her mind repeated the fortune's message, over and over again, on a never-ending loop. It was in Renteria's voice. It was coming from him.

(touch it)
(touch it)
(touch it)

Before she had crossed the threshold, she heard Kim say she didn't understand—the small ribbon was blank, nothing of significance there at all, nothing to worry about. Which was impossible because Amanda had seen what was written there, and the message was very clear.

TOUCH IT, the small ribbon had read, and she had never felt colder, more haunted, in all her life.

7

TEN MINUTES LATER, the power came back on, shutting off the emergency lights and shrinking the darkness throughout the entire facility. The patients were stuck in the same positions they'd been when the lights had cut off. Not a single nurse reported movement among them. Manuel Renteria was the only one who held that honor, and why that was, Amanda couldn't fathom. Couldn't possibly guess. There were a great many things happening at Spring Lakes that she couldn't explain through science or logic, and why the man had suddenly stood up was currently chief among them.

He's here to haunt me.

That was the best she could do given the circumstances, and, to her, it made the most sense. The old man looked so much like her grandfather she'd thought it *was* him. He had that same wooly mustache, the little dark gray curls that rested atop his narrow head. A skinny, lanky man, not an ounce of fat on him. The sweet aroma of cigarillos he wore in lieu of cologne. His awful breath, that combination of smoke and advanced halitosis. The resemblance freaked her out, so much so she found it hard to concentrate on anything, including the task at hand—to find out what the hell was going down in the Garden State.

She was in the security office going over the footage from the blackout. There weren't any cameras in the rooms (*privacy laws* Kim had explained) so she couldn't replay what had happened inside Renteria's dorm. She scanned the main common room to see if any of the nurses had been wrong, if one of the other patients had moved before or after the blackout. Not that any of this would help her prove her wild theories, but still—she needed to know if Renteria's case was an isolated one.

She needed to know if this thing—whatever it was—was after her.

A silly notion, she knew, but her mind started piecing together the evidence, and the strangeness of it all lent itself to such thoughts. She couldn't help it.

She looked at the room from various angles. There was no movement among the sixty-niners, and they were stationed where they had been since the sickness had taken over. If she synched up the footage from earlier, it would reveal no differences. She fast-forwarded the tape until she passed the blackout, when the emergency lights had kicked on. She watched the nurses scramble around the room, panicking as they attended to the non-sixty-niners, those who hadn't been evacuated yet.

Soon, Kim had promised her, *the buses are on the way.*

As the nurses took care of those who were more alive than dead, Amanda zoomed in on the frozen faces. She studied each of them, playing the same three minutes of footage over and over again. They remained still. Not one of them so much as twitched. There were no involuntary muscle spasms. The patients were obedient and consistent with their previous symptoms, unlike Manuel Renteria.

That was until she came across a woman sitting in the corner of the common room all by her lonesome, the sixty-niner who'd had her nose in a book, and had (probably) been rocking before the thing that happened had rendered her body stiff and impossibly heavy. Her eyes were no longer focused on the words in front of her since the paperback had hit the ground and now lay at her feet. They were turned toward the ceiling as if the story were scrawled above her. Her mouth was slightly open, just more than a crack, enough so Amanda could spot the darkness within. She recalled the awful footage from earlier, the thirty-second clip that showed the transformation, captured the woman writhing and violently convulsing, her limbs twisting without her approval. And that was when the movement happened; the pixelated area near the woman's mouth jumped.

It was slight, just a blip. But enough to drag Amanda away from her meandering thoughts. No one who'd been in the room, not one of the three nurses, would have noticed it unless their eyes were trained on the woman's lips. With all the bustle and panic that had transpired, no one had the time to pay any attention to those rendered completely motionless. Amanda had the luxury of instant replay. She rewound the footage and watched again. Studied the pixels as they blipped and blinked. She zoomed out and watched again but wasn't able to learn anything new. Then she switched camera angles, zoomed back in on the woman's mouth.

She saw something sweep the opening, something white. Something that contrasted the darkness. It was long and thin, a straw-like whisker. But it curled, traveled sideways along the woman's lips in a sweeping motion, probing the open area past her flesh. Almost like a... like a...

She didn't want to speak it aloud, nor did she want to give the thoughts any plausibility because of how ridiculous it sounded. But the object did look like a flexible antenna, reminding her of some crustacean. Or what it really looked like was an insect leg, which seemed pretty gross and pretty impossible that an insect that large would have inhabited the woman's mouth without someone noticing, and she was certain her mind was just making shit up now because she couldn't rationalize a single iota of everything that had happened.

But, as she played the clip over and over again, her mind couldn't come up with better conjectures. A grasshopper leg (possibly the world's longest, if indeed it was one), or some insect equivalent, a thin hairless appendage designed to jump, propel the bulk of its owner into the air and take flight. It was living inside the old woman, staked a claim to her oral domain.

Her skin crawled.

What the hell am I seeing?

She wished she knew.

What the hell is happening here?

She had no idea, but she was determined to find out.

8

PHELPS LIT A smoke for them. She'd been good that day, had only smoked one since landing in New Jersey. Quitting was tough business though, and, after what had happened in Renteria's room, the craving had intensified, set her nerves on fire.

The first drag was always the best, the way the smoke hit her lungs, filling her with that necessary poison, sending the sensation on a magic carpet ride through her bloodstream, scratching at that temporary euphoric state. She enjoyed the first drag, the second too, holding them in her lungs far longer than she would the rest. After, she passed the cigarette to Barnes, who took it slowly, put the tan end between his lips, and inhaled. He was a casual smoker, had quit a long time ago when he had kicked the bottle, but borrowed a smoke every once in a while. He'd never been coy about his past and his struggles with alcoholism, though Phelps had never pried information from him. She wasn't much for gossip and didn't know Barnes that well, had never felt comfortable asking, but over the past few month things had changed and the two had become pretty close co-workers.

"Okay," she said, taking the smoke back from him. "I have to ask. And you don't have to answer if you don't want to."

Barnes looked at her dubiously, exhaling a cloud between them. "Oh God. This oughta be a good one."

"You quit smoking when you quit drinking, right?"

"Yep."

"Doesn't smoking... I dunno... make you want it again?"

He squinted as if thinking about the answer gave him a headache. "No, not really. Although they fall under the same category, I suppose, nicotine and alcohol, my brain is able to separate the two. I don't have any desire to drink again. Smoke every once in a while. And, honestly, I don't even enjoy it as much as I used to. Sometimes a cigarette tastes like shit."

"That's weird." She took in another lungful, then released a thick fog. It most certainly did not taste like shit. "I enjoy it too much. I've tried to quit. Like a hundred times. Patches, pills—none of them work. It's the *want* I think. I *want* to smoke. I've convinced myself I'll be a smoker forever."

Barnes shrugged. "I wanted to drink. A lot. All the time, actually. Never wanted to spend a minute of my day sober. It was wired into my brain, that line of thinking. That constant *want*. It was habitual. After a while, your body convinces you that you *need* it, and that's where the real internal war is waged."

She shook her head, unable to relate. Sure, she thought about smoking when she wasn't. But not every single waking moment. It was there when she wanted it. On her breaks. After lunch, after dinner. With that cup of coffee on the drive to work. The smokes were a companion and she never felt like she *needed* it—it was just something that was certain. Always there. Ever present. A part of her.

"Any tips?" she asked, as she burned through more paper and tobacco.

"On quitting?" Barnes shrugged again, offered her a contagious smile. "First you have to want to."

"Ah, therein lies my problem."

"Indeed. Convincing yourself that don't need it, or don't want it, is the hardest part of the process. The physical symptoms are nothing compared to the mental ones. Anyone can beat a sickness, the flu or a cold—but not everyone can defeat their own mind."

"Hm. Some sage-like advice right there."

He plucked the cigarette out of her hand. There wasn't much left, but he took the rest of it down to the filter, then tossed the butt into the parking lot.

"I think you could do it, Phelps. Quit, I mean. You might just learn something about yourself."

"You think so?" She fingered the top of her pack, *wanting* to snatch another one, stick it between her lips and light up. The shared cigarette didn't ease her nerves as much as she'd thought and she had convinced herself a second one would do the trick. She squeezed the filter of another cig, but something stopped her from pulling it free.

"I do," he said, walking toward the parking lot, as if something had caught his attention. "The mind—it's a powerful tool. The most powerful tool on the planet if you ask me. It has the ability to make us great..." She eyed him as he walked farther, weaving between the sea of parked cars. "Or destroy us."

"Where are you going?" she asked, closing the pack and pocketing them.

He drifted across the parking lot, toward the back where a patch of woods bordered the entire facility. How long the woods went on for, Phelps didn't know. It looked endless from their vantage point, but so do a lot of forests at the beginning. Could have gone on for miles or just a few hundred feet. There was no way to tell.

She followed him, slowly, wondering where he was going and why he wasn't answering her.

"Barnes?" she asked, scoffing. "What the hell, man?"

Barnes stopped short of the forest. He bent down on one knee. There was something on the small strip of grass between the woods and the lot. Something turquoise. Long. It was sparkly, even beneath the cloudy sky that had fallen over them.

"What is it?" Phelps asked, hurrying over.

"Phelps?"

"What?" She hated the sound of his voice. The alarm in his tone spiked her heart rate. "What is it?"

"There are seven of them, aren't there? The sixty-niners?"

"Yeah, that's what we counted. Why?"

Holding the object up, he turned to her. It was a scarf, a thin fashion accessory that hardly provided any warmth. "Because I think we might be missing one."

9

"HOW COULD THIS happen?" Kim Charon questioned no one in particular. Her hands were at her temples and she twisted her lips, a rage burning strong within her.

Amanda approached her like a stick of dynamite. "It must have happened when the lights went out." Providing a reasonable answer wasn't going to make things better, but at least it was an excuse. The woman had slipped out, undetected, during the outage. "It's all on tape if you want to see."

"And no one saw her leave?" Kim's hands fell on her hips. "Not a single one of the CNAs or the assistants?"

Amanda looked to Phelps and Barnes, both of whom had directed their eyes elsewhere—the floor, the ceiling, anywhere but the unpleasant woman's hard gaze.

"Mrs. Charon, I believe if you review the tape—"

"What? What is it?"

"Well, it's really odd. Might be better just to show you."

Kim threw her hands up in surrender. "Fine. Show me. Better explain why a sixty-nine-year-old woman with chronic back pain was able to get up and find her way out the door in the dark *without* a single person in this goddamn facility noticing her."

Oh, it will, Amanda thought. *Ohhhhh it will.*

They crammed into the security office. Amanda had left the clip on the screen, paused on the exact moment before the lights went out. Julie Finch was stationed in a rocking chair, near the front door. They could see the window behind her with clarity.

Without saying a word, without prefacing the footage, Amanda pressed play.

The screen went dark. On the tape, the lights flickered for a second, and, in that blip, they saw Julie Finch was standing, her entire body turned toward the camera. Her lips spread apart, displaying the black hole that was her mouth. Her eyes were wide open, nearly popping out of her skull, as if someone were squeezing her, choking her, *killing her.* The image was gone in a blink and the screen went dark again. Then the emergency lights kicked on, throwing sepia shadows over the room.

The woman was gone.

The window was open.

No matter how many times Amanda watched the footage, a strong case of the chills washed over her, hardening her flesh. Her blood ran cold. Her neck tingled with a haunted touch. She wanted to shed her skin just to rid herself of the feeling.

For a solid ten seconds, no one in the office spoke a word.

Then, Kim stood up straight, lifting her chin with authority. "Well. Does anyone want to provide a rational explanation on how a sixty-nine-year-old woman with a terrible back, advanced arthritis, and degenerative muscle tone can lift open a window and climb through it, all in the matter of a few seconds?"

It was a question no one had an answer for, not a logical one. Amanda kept coming back to *The Exorcist* movie, but an answer of that nature was sure to get her thrown out of here, and, if her superiors caught wind of it, they'd probably—at the very least—document her.

"No," was the answer Amanda settled on, and it was the truest answer she could currently provide. It was simple, and it was accurate. "There is no logical explanation for this. Nor the note that was tucked in the back of Manuel Renteria's throat."

"You mean the blank piece of paper?"

Blank to you, Amanda thought, but dared not speak.

"Yes, the blank piece of paper." She watched Barnes's eyes lock onto hers when she spoke those words. She didn't know what he was trying to tell her, but *just shut it* was probably close enough.

"I think the important thing is," Barnes said, putting his hands on his hips and pacing the small office, "that we find her. Quickly. Without making a big fuss of it."

"You mean," Kim said, directing her awful stare at him, "without notifying certain authorities."

Barnes seemed hesitant to respond. "I think that would be a bigger mess than what we need right now. Luckily, no one has tipped off the local news outlets. Or dealing with this issue with discretion would be an impossibility. I think we should take the opportunity to find Mrs. Finch before this whole thing blows up. And the sooner we get out there looking, the sooner we can bring her back without causing a media circus for the duration of our investigation."

"For once, I actually agree with you." Kim nodded. Her lawyers kept unusually quiet, uncharacteristically still. They kept their distance from her, as if the woman were a wild, unpredictable animal that could strike at any moment. Occasionally they glanced down at their phones, probably wishing to receive some important call, something to drag them away from this escalating situation. Something that would free them from this nonsense.

This frightening nonsense, Amanda thought.

"Good. It's settled then." Barnes spun and faced Amanda. "I'll head into the woods and track her down."

"Well, I'm coming with you."

"Me too," Phelps added, stepping forward.

Amanda nodded. There was no way they were staying behind and dealing with the woman and her attitude alone.

Barnes turned toward Kim. "We'll need a representative from the facility to accompany us. A guard preferably. In case Mrs. Finch isn't... *cooperative.*"

The woman nodded. "I'll stick Cunningham on it."

"Sounds good. Tell Mr. Cunningham to be ready in five."

Kim craned her head toward Amanda. "What am I supposed to do in the meantime?"

Amanda gave her that *what-you-should-have-done-already* glance and folded her arms. "Get the rest of these people out of here. Send your staff home except for one CNA and one guard." She paused, pinching her lower lip between her teeth. "This facility isn't safe anymore."

10

CUNNINGHAM WAS TALL, but he didn't have a lot of muscle on him, and that wasn't comforting to the others. Not that the man needed to look like Rambo to take down an old lady if she got agitated and violent, but still—he wasn't built like your typical security guard, capable of handling messy situations or physical altercations. Amanda had seen mall cops strike a more authoritative pose. Alas, he was the one Kim had stuck them with, and it wasn't like they had much of a choice; Cunningham was one of two on duty.

Their parade crunched through the wooded area, snapping twigs and branches that had fallen during the last storm. The path was narrow but easily navigated. As they moved through the woodland, Amanda was stricken with a certain sense of dread, a foreboding that caused her muscles to tighten and cramp with discomfort. A trickle of sweat ran down her back.

"How much farther before we give up and head back?" Amanda asked Barnes, as if he were the one in charge now. He'd seemed to have inherited the role of leader when he had suggested they embark on this little escapade. Even though she knew she still called the shots and could steer them home any time she wanted. It was fun letting Barnes lead them. In fact, it eased her nerves a bit. Being in charge all the time placed a lot of pressure on her shoulders, and since they'd come to Spring Lakes and had dealt with its mega-bitch director, she felt there was no escaping from that demanding role. It was good to climb into the back seat, let someone else drive awhile.

"Just a little farther," Barnes replied, stepping over a tree that had fallen across the path.

They'd already been hiking for ten minutes, and the woods were getting thicker. The foliage was beginning to take over the path, and Amanda found herself brushing away hanging vines and leafy arms every fifteen steps or so. She wondered if there would still be a path in another fifteen minutes. That, and the graying skies, provided some anxious concern. She could smell the dampness in the air, the earthly musk, and the threat of rainfall, a heavy, sky-opening downpour, quickly became very possible. Not that a little water bothered her, but she hadn't brought extra clothes, had left her bags at the hotel, and she didn't feel like spending the rest of the day feeling like a soggy cocoon.

Just when their route had become overcrowded with branches and clusters of drooping vegetation, they saw a break ahead—a field lit up by an afternoon sun that had begun to poke through the cloud-congested skies. She saw where the straw grass met the tree line and began to feel a little better about their situation; although, there was no sign of their missing guest. They hadn't discovered another garment during their trek even though Barnes had claimed to see the woman's footsteps in the mud, evidence she'd come this far, which had been the only reason Amanda had allowed them to continue their pursuit.

They exited the woods and entered the field. Amanda felt the straw grass brush against her pant legs, and she headed toward the center of the field where the grass had died some time ago, the circular shape reduced to a bed of dead, yellow straw and powdery dirt. She thought she saw something out there, something colorful that contrasted the yellowish tinge of the hip-high grass. Something...

Turquoise.

As they approached, the scene took form. A woman in a greenish-blue sweater was kneeling, praying before an altar that wasn't there. Amanda saw nothing before her, no religious statues of any kind. There was nothing but the circular area in the middle of the tall grass, a small void that someone had carved into nature.

Someone had to have done this, she thought. It couldn't have formed naturally, the circular shape that was stamped into the middle of the field. She was quickly reminded of crop circles, the kind she'd seen on TV specials and movies, the kind in real life that were often done by pranksters and ancient-alien wackadoodles. She looked to the sky as if answers were scribbled among the parting clouds, but, of course, there was nothing written there save for the bleak promise of sunshine and natural warmth.

That sinking feeling returned, and the bottom of her stomach plummeted. She knew they shouldn't have come here without the authorities, an official witness to all the bad things that were sure to come.

We shouldn't be here, she thought. *It's not too late to turn around. Call the cops. Let them deal with this.*

But they didn't turn around. Didn't call the cops. Didn't let someone else deal with the situation at hand. Barnes led them to the fringe, where the straw grass ended, and the giant circle of dirt and dead vegetation began. Amanda's stomach rolled. Uneasiness gripped her shoulders. Her bones filled with anxiety, a cool rush of apprehension.

She had a clear view now. The missing guest, Julie Finch, was kneeling before an object, about the size of a refrigerator, that was halfway embedded in the dirt. There were five small stones around it, placed in a circular pattern and spread evenly apart. The object in the center was disc-like, coated in a gunmetal shell. It looked like a rock, the rocky and rough exterior providing no definite shape, even though it appeared ovoid.

Amanda's entire body felt on fire, trepidation burning up her nerves.

What the hell is this?

The lost woman mumbled something, repeating the expression over and over, but it was in a language foreign to Amanda's ears. Sounded more like syllables than words. From the looks on everyone's faces, no one else recognized the jargon either.

"Mrs. Finch?" Cunningham asked, his voice cracking. He took a reluctant step toward her, his hand gliding toward his belt where he had a small baton. Amanda wanted to protest even the thought of using a weapon in this situation, but she couldn't locate her voice. Cunningham continued, picking up his pace, and his confidence. "Mrs. Finch, I think you better come back to the facility with us. Everyone's real worried about you. Especially Mrs. Charon."

The woman ended her strange mantra. She didn't turn around. Instead, she kept her focus on the object in the dirt, that circular thing that looked like a giant quarter, only not as smooth.

Then the surrounding stones began to glow. Purple at first, but then the color changed, blending in shades of pink. Then blue. Dabbles of orange and red. Magenta and fuchsia streaks. The stones cycled through a myriad of colors before they stopped, burned out and were reduced to a lifeless gray again. The five rocks, which seemed misplaced in this world, sat half-buried in the dirt as if they hadn't been glowing only moments ago.

Amanda watched Mrs. Finch carefully, expecting her to do something, to carry on with whatever she'd escaped here to do. To say something. Anything. But instead the woman kept completely still, frozen, like she'd been at Spring Lakes, doing her best imitation of a tree, some inanimate object that existed in nature. Continuing to face the mysterious object embedded in the field, she didn't move a muscle. Didn't flinch. Kept her focus on the abnormal formation before her.

A shiver rifled through Amanda's body, and she suddenly felt foreign in her own skin.

"Mrs. Finch?" Cunningham asked, moving closer to the woman and the stones. Within a couple seconds he was right behind the sixty-nine-year-old woman, his shadow closing over her. "Mrs. Finch, I really think we oughta—"

The thing in the dirt made a strange noise, a loud braying noise that sounded like a broken car horn. At least, Amanda thought that was where the sound had come from. She supposed it could have come from the sky or somewhere deep in the forest. But it was too loud to have come from those places. The noise was close. Too close. She considered the possibility that the woman had vocalized the harsh sound, but nothing human could be responsible for such an awful racket. The drawn-out honking was dominant, forcing Amanda to cover her ears. The entire group followed suit, clapping their hands against the sides of their heads, their faces strained with worry and pain. Phelps closed her eyes and dropped to her knees. Cunningham walked backward on his heels and collapsed after he'd taken a few steps. He writhed on the ground, the sound too much for his head to handle. Barnes kept his footing, but he too pinched shut his eyes, bracing against that awful noise. He grimaced as the sound droned on for all the world to hear.

The old woman didn't seem to mind the noise. In fact, she seemed to embrace it. Her body rocked from side to side, as if she was swaying along to some pleasant tune's catchy rhythm. Amanda couldn't see her face, but she pictured the woman smiling as she let the awful din fill her ears, carry her off to some delightful mental space.

Amanda's head began to ache, the pain dull at first, but, as the never-ending out-of-tune trumpet sound dragged on, it grew to be much worse. Like someone had her head in a vice and the two sides were ratcheting down. The discomfort developed over the next few seconds, got so bad she envisioned her head exploding, popping under the pressure. She fought off the pain and the ridiculous notions, forcing herself to believe it wasn't that bad and it would all end soon. Then she closed her eyes, begging for the constant pressure to end, making deals with gods she had never believed in.

When she opened her eyes again, it was night.

Huh? What?

In two seconds, the world had changed. It'd gone from light to dark in the snap of two fingers, and Amanda's brain couldn't process it, couldn't accept this shift in reality. She shook her head, unable to commit to the idea of losing several hours over the course of a few seconds. The time shift had sent her into a daze and the world slipped before her, her vision tilting askew. She blinked, hoping to return to the past where things made sense, where *time* made sense. When that didn't work, she smacked the side of her head several times with the heels of her palms, hoping to reset her vision. But no, the sky continued to cloak itself with the dark, an endless starry expanse revealing the cosmic roadmap of the entire solar system.

This can't be.

But it was. And here she was, under the night's sky, in the middle of the field that felt hundreds of thousands of miles away from where she'd been only moments ago.

Around her feet, her companions knelt in the dirt. They weren't moving. They were still just like the woman had been prior to the strange sound. Just like the sixty-niners of Spring Lakes, stiff and trance-like. Their eyes were settled on the thing in the dirt, only, that was gone too. It was all dirt now, a small mound of powdery brown. Nothing unusual about it. The stones that had been there were gone too. Just dirt and matted straw grass, as if something big had lived here for a long time. Something enormous. Something circular.

Her mind raced. She turned to the group. Their eyes were closed now; despite clenching them shut, red streams dribbled down their faces, the blood flowing steadily onto the earthen pad before them. Their mouths were in motion, though, their lips moved so quickly Amanda could barely make out a word. She surmised they probably weren't speaking English anyway, but some indecipherable alien language instead. She picked up on the same syllables being recited over and over, like a prayer. A foreign mantra. An exotic narrative that made zero sense. Silent whispers in the dark of night. The peculiar vocalizations coming from the old woman, the young security guard, and the only two people here she truly trusted made Amanda's body break out in gooseflesh. Her head crawled as a horde of invisible insects scurried across her scalp.

She faced the center of the circle. In place of the disc-like object was now a man. A tall man. Impossibly tall, perhaps the tallest human being she'd ever seen in real life. His arms were long, almost *too* long, bent awkwardly in places, as if he had some bone disease, and his fingers—they were long too, gnarled with a severe case of something akin to advanced rheumatoid arthritis. The knuckles were so swollen they looked like flesh-covered golf balls.

His face, however, was perhaps the most normal thing about him, and it was very, *very* recognizable.

"*Hello there,* pequeña," the man said, his voice roughened from decades' worth of hard boozing and an out-of-control cigarette habit. "*So glad you could make it.*"

She removed her hands away from the sides of her head, found that awful noise had faded into obscurity.

Now she could focus on the face before her. She gave her companions one last glance, saw their mouths twitching in sync with each other, reciting their chilling prayer until the end of time would come, until the hand of doom would come sweep them off their feet and carry them toward an elegant oblivion. The blood leaked more freely now that their eyes had opened, freshets of crimson pouring down their faces like a new spill, pooling in the dirt around their knees.

She told herself this wasn't real. It didn't *feel* real, so, therefore, she convinced herself it wasn't.

An illusion. It had to be. Some fucked up daydream.

Day-*night*-dream.

"So glad you could join us."

"You're not him," was the first thing she said to it, and it was an *it*. *It* had to be. There was nothing else she could call it. Though it wore flesh and clothes—a Sunday's best special—it had no right to call itself *human*. The thing before her was disjointed, a novice's attempt at hammering down the human anatomy. Disproportionate appendages. A face that was more bone than skin. A gangly frame that stood eight to nine feet off the ground. Her grandfather hadn't been anywhere near that tall.

This was not him.

Just a terrifying imitation.

"Of course, it is. I'm him. Oh, I am, I am, I am."

Behind him, the trees moved, though there was no wind to speak of. It was as if something giant were lurking in the brush, pacing back and forth near the tree line like an attack dog waiting to be free from its kennel. The oaks swayed; their branches bending violently in the still, starry backdrop.

"No," she said confidently. "You're not him. And this... this isn't real."

The thing pretending to be Grandpa Guerrero frowned like a despondent clown. *"Why must you say such painful things? I'm real. So is this place. Everything you see here is one hundred percent real. Everything you see is sixty-nine."*

Sixty-nine?

She thought she had heard that last part wrong, but deep down, she knew she hadn't. He'd said that number, and he'd *meant* it.

Sixty-nine. He had said 'everything is sixty-nine.'

"What is sixty-nine?" she asked, without giving it much thought. An instinctive reaction to her begotten curiosity. "What's the significance of that number?"

Her grandfather, or rather, the thing that wore his appearance like a new coat, grinned devilishly. Its crooked fingers caressed its pale face, and the hideous figure seemed genuinely delighted that the question had been proposed. Giddy almost. *"Sixty-nine is everything!"* it said with glee.

She didn't understand but she knew that was the point. She wasn't meant to understand, comprehend what the orchestrator of this nightmare was trying to convey. Not this way. This thing, she doubted, held any answers. Only riddles.

There were other things she wanted to ask before it all went away, before the dream collapsed and sent her spiraling back toward reality. But movement beyond the field, the way the trees arced and whipped on the dark that bordered this place, held her attention.

The answers to the riddles of this place were there, she thought, beyond the field.

Where the giant horror roamed.

She faced the grandfather-thing. His face had already begun to change, its faux skin melting like soft candy under the sun. Its wrinkles twisted and its flesh fell away, revealing the pink tissue beneath its mask. Its eyes expanded and then almost simultaneously contracted, as if they didn't know what size they wanted to be. Boils began to form on its face, pulsing, threatening to explode with infectious, disease-carrying filth.

"Sixty-nine!" the thing barked. *"Sixty-nine! Sixty-nine!"*

Its jaw unhinged, broke off on one side, disconnecting near its left earlobe. It swung free. Still, the creature was able to speak with a clarity that pulled the plug on Amanda's current understanding of actuality.

"Sixty-nine! Sixty-nine! Sixty-nine!"

It lunged forward, swinging its boneless arms wildly. They moved like ropes, loose and undulating, with the grace of a habitual drunkard.

It came for her.

She screamed.

Closed her eyes.

Opened them.

Daylight flooded her vision. She was on her back, facing the sky, the warmth of the afternoon toasting her skin. Flipping over, onto her hands and knees, she surveyed the area, wondering if the others were okay, if they'd seen what she'd seen, or if the grand illusion had been too much for them to handle. Because it *was* an illusion; it had to be.

There was a commotion.

Barnes and Phelps were crouched over Cunningham. The kid was screaming, holding his face, clawing at his flesh. She could see blood, a glistening red mask that covered most of his features. His cries were shrill, and, like a colicky infant, there was no consoling him. Barnes and Phelps were trying their best to quiet him, holding him down and shushing him. His arms began flailing all over the place, his legs kicking, lashing out against whatever invisible monsters plagued him. They told him they couldn't help if he kept jerking around. Just then, he bolted up and Amanda got a good glimpse at his face—what was left of it—and the horrors it held.

His eyes were *gone*. In their places were two scarlet trenches, two tunnels that led into the depths of his skull. They were filled with blood. Two red rivers poured down his face, soaking the front of his uniform.

The kid screamed again, screamed until his vocal cords splintered.

And Amanda heard someone laughing. A low, pleased giggle that set a wave of shivers across her neck. She turned and saw Julie Finch sitting in the center of the circle, cross-legged, watching the scene unfold, a joyous expression capturing her face. Her whole body hitched as she suddenly exploded with uproarious laughter. She cackled at the bright sky.

Her eyes glazed over, a cloudy-white film taking full control.

Something poked out of the woman's mouth, and Amanda knew exactly what it was the second it happened—the leg of a grasshopper, some insect-like appendage, pushing its insect body past the tongue, farther into the woman's gullet.

Into her soul.

II

AFTER THE AMBULANCE left, with Cunningham, for the hospital, after Mrs. Finch had been heavily sedated and quarantined, the police had questions. A small crowd had formed around the facility, no more than fifteen people, nosy onlookers who had heard whispers of a peculiar situation unfolding at Spring Lakes, locals who had come running once the flashing lights and sirens were seen and heard. A reporter from a local rag dropped by, but she was turned away by the police presence and was forced to remain a member of the undistinguished crowd.

Barnes and Amanda had told the cops everything. Well, not *everything*. But close enough. They told them about the garment they'd found near the entrance of the woods and that they had thought they could bring back Mrs. Finch easily, without the aid of law enforcement, especially since they had believed she hadn't gotten very far. They had gone to the end of the path where they had found the field and had discovered Mrs. Finch in the center of it, praying. It was weird, borderline bizarre, but she was pre-Alzheimer's, so they had thought nothing of it at the time. Maybe she was confused, maybe she thought she was back in church or receiving some holy sacrament. Amanda told the cops she hadn't speculated about what the woman was doing out there, that their only intent was to bring her back safely. They had tried to help her off the ground when...

"He just lost it," Barnes told the officer writing the statement. "Started clawing at his eyes. His face. It was... it was horrible."

"What made him do it?" asked the cop.

Barnes never looked away, his eyes never faltering. He'd prepared his lies well and did a surprisingly convincing job delivering them. If the whole CDC thing didn't work out, Amanda would encourage Barnes to pursue a career in Hollywood. "I have no idea. He... just went mad."

The cop didn't look like he believed him, but Amanda and Phelps were there to corroborate, which gave credence to Barnes's tale.

"Can you show me the field?" the cop asked. He turned to his buddy, as if he was expecting the big-bellied man to object. "I'd like to see it." His partner nodded without any spirit.

"Sure thing."

Barnes led the two cops down the path. This time, the whole crew came along save for the nursing staff. Kim Charon and her two pet lawyers insisted they tag along, and despite the cops suggesting how unnecessary their presence was, they came anyway. Kim was very convincing and made her case, though she had taken a much more delicate approach with the officers than she had Amanda and her team.

When they reached the end of the path, there was no field. Just more path, ruled by overgrowth and downed timber.

"I don't understand," Barnes said, scanning the woods with disbelief. The path before them narrowed so much they couldn't pass through without risking someone twisting an ankle or breaking a foot. Too many uprooted trees, too much uneven terrain. "It was right here."

The cops looked at each other. "Maybe you took a wrong turn somewhere," said the one with the belly.

Barnes looked appreciative of the cop's gesture. He'd wasted their time bringing them out here, yet, the officer didn't give him a hard time. "Yeah," Barnes said, hugging himself, *comforting* himself. "Yeah, maybe. Wrong turn."

But there were no turns. It had been a straight shot and Barnes knew that. Amanda knew that. And Phelps knew that too. Despite this knowledge, their eyes weren't deceiving them. The path ended, here, in the middle of the woods.

The field simply didn't exist.

When they got back to Spring Lakes, the cops told them they'd review what happened, investigate and keep everyone updated on Cunningham. They allowed the CDC workers to continue their own investigation into the sixty-niner situation; though, they did recommend having a police presence to preside over the process in case "something like this happens again."

"It's just... safer," one of the officers said. "We'll have the precinct send someone over. You'll want help controlling the media once they get hold of it. We already turned away *one* local reporter."

Amanda didn't disagree. It *was* safer. Especially considering what the three of them had witnessed.

After the cops left, they found themselves in Kim's office. Her eyes were wide and wild, filled with absolute anger.

"Do you three want to tell me what *the hell* happened out there? For real?"

No one spoke up.

Amanda checked her watch. It must've broken sometime during their excursion, stopped and restarted after they'd left the woods. The clock claimed only an hour had passed since their departure, and their first trip into the woods had taken at least that. Probably more.

"How long were we gone?" she asked, noticing the hands on the clock above the door matched the one on her wrist. "The first time. When we located Mrs. Finch. How long did that whole ordeal take?"

Kim shrugged, looking to her lawyers for verification. "Ten minutes. No more. Very quick, which is what makes this whole Cunningham thing a hard pill to swallow. Why?"

Amanda gulped, louder than expected. "Just seemed longer, I guess." She glanced over at Barnes and Phelps, and they stared back as if they were thinking the same damn thing—*this is utterly impossible. We were out there for at least an hour, maybe two.*

Barnes got up and stormed out of the office.

"Where does he think he's going?" Kim asked. She was pissed, and, as much as Amanda had grown to despise her, she couldn't blame her for getting upset. This whole clusterfuck had snowballed into a bigger clusterfuck, and things weren't promising to get better, or easier, anytime soon.

"Our other team should be arriving shortly," she said, which wasn't a complete lie. They should have landed in Newark over an hour ago and been halfway down the shore by now. "Barnes probably went to call our superior, Denny Cohen, and get a better ETA. They'll have more equipment and tests we can run on the guests."

This didn't seem to satisfy the woman. Her upper lip squirmed. "Tests. More tests."

"Yes, ma'am. Being the initial investigation unit, we're a little bit limited with our supplies. The next team will have everything we need."

"What's our next step then? Wait around, hoping your friends get here? We've evacuated almost everyone like you asked. Less than ten guests are waiting to be picked up by their families. I have two nurses and one guard left on staff. I'm about to send them both home as well." She tapped her forehead with the heel of her palm. "Jesus Christ, Cunningham. That poor young man's face..." She turned her head, disgusted, as if

Amanda's face were a shiny sheet of red and her eyes had mysteriously been plucked from their sockets.

"What happened was very tragic. I wish I had some sort of explanation for what happened out there, I really do."

"I wish you did too, Mrs. Guerrero. I wish you did too. But you don't. In fact, since you've arrived, conditions have worsened. All your tests and experiments have been a complete failure. You don't know any more about this thing now than when you first got here."

"This thing," she said, leaning forward, "is unprecedented. Whatever is happening here is going to take more than my team and a few machines to figure out. This is... this is unheard of in the medical field. An anomaly. Scientifically, I can't explain these... *things.* I can't explain why there was a note tucked in the back of Manuel Renteria's throat."

"A *blank* piece of paper, you mean."

She wanted to tell her. Took everything in her power to dance around the truth. She let the comment go, chose to ignore it.

"I can't tell you what truly happened to Cunningham because I have no idea what compelled him to harm himself. *No* idea."

Kim turned to stone. Her eyes fixed on Amanda, never wavered. It was like she was trying to see the truth behind her strong facade, but the truth was exactly what Amanda presented—even though she knew a little more than she had let on, the fact was, she didn't know everything. Hadn't the slightest clue as to what was going down at Spring Lakes and the surrounding woods.

The Field.

Whatever it is, The Field is the source of it.

"The things we've witnessed this morning, Mrs. Charon, they make *zero* sense."

She didn't realize how manic she sounded until she saw how Kim and her lawyers were staring at her. Even

Phelps, who'd been directly touched by today's events, viewed her curiously. She shot her a *stop-losing-your-shit* look, and Amanda cleared her expression with her right hand, took a step back, and propped herself against the wall. She was done talking, explaining herself to Kim and her legal team.

Talking, at this point, was counterproductive.

I am losing my shit, Amanda thought. *I'm totally losing my shit.*

She kept seeing that creature in the field, the one that looked like her dead grandfather. The way its arms moved, the bones beneath its flesh nonexistent. Two long appendages filled with jelly, flopping around as the body propelled itself forward, after her. Reaching. Its pallid face gleaming in the moonlit glow. That smile, those crooked teeth. The bulge in its pants, protruding like some dangerous weapon, available and accessible in the face of immediate peril. Like the small baton Cunningham had almost used on Mrs. Fields, probably would have too (maybe) if the world hadn't suddenly turned itself upside down, if the kid hadn't gone and torn out his own eyes.

If that was what he'd done.

(touch it)

(go ahead)

(it won't hurt)

(touch it)

She shuddered.

"Are you okay, Mrs. Guerrero?" Kim asked, folding her hands on her desk.

"Yes. I'm fine."

"You don't look fine."

"I just need some fresh air."

"Go get some. And when you're done, for the love of Christ, can you please tell me what the fuck is happening inside my facility? Is that too much to ask?"

She made no promises and left the office without speaking another word. She headed for the back door. She felt a certain darkness follow her, the same darkness she'd experienced among the dead grass and endless forest.

12

AMANDA CLIMBED OUT of the Uber and thanked the driver, then faced Curly's Pub, a small, dingy joint just off the highway and located about two miles from Spring Lakes. She hurried inside without delay, checking her phone incessantly, impatiently waiting for updates from her boss, Denny Cohen. As soon as she passed through the entrance, she spotted Barnes at the bar, one of three people sitting bellies to the bar top and nursing their favorite drinks. He saw her immediately and laughed a little when their eyes met. She didn't find their predicament so comical.

"Tracking the GPS in my phone?" Barnes asked as she came over. "Don't remember that being in the employee handbook."

She grimaced. "Didn't need a tracker to find you."

"Am I that predictable?"

She took the stool next to him. "I thought you quit. What the fuck are you doing?"

"I did quit." He stirred the contents of his dark drink, what looked like vodka and coke. She couldn't smell the alcohol on him to be sure, but, if she had to wager, that was what she'd put her money on.

The bartender came over and asked Amanda what her poison was, to which she replied, "Water, thank you." He poured her a water on the spot, and, when he was finished, after he had left to restock the lemons and limes, she turned to her employee.

"Do you want to talk about it?" she asked, keeping her voice low. The nature of their conversation wasn't meant for anyone else's ears, especially a couple of barflies with a few drinks in them. Who knew what complications that might spark? No one needed to hear about what had happened out in the field, the terrors that had taken place there. That was their secret, their experience, and she intended to share it with no one.

(touch it)

In other words, today was not the day she wanted to get fitted for a straitjacket.

"We can talk about it. About what happened in the field."

"So, you saw things out there, too?" he asked, seeming to already know the answer.

"Of course, I saw the field."

On the surface, he smiled, perhaps a direct result of the drinks he'd consumed before she had reached him. But, behind his good humor, she could tell the fear had gripped him, a sizable amount that ate away at his confidence, gnawed his nerves down to nothing. "Well, the cops didn't see it. It... it disappeared. Hid from us. It's like... it was playing a game with us." His head tilted to the side. "I'm sounding crazy, aren't I?" She didn't answer, even though similar thoughts had passed through her. "Tell me—how the hell does a field disappear like that?"

"I don't know, Barnes. I don't know any more about this than you do. But you know what—we'll figure it out together. You don't have to do *this*." She tapped the bar top next to his drink. "You don't have to ruin your sobriety. Don't let a few hallucinations destroy everything you've worked so hard for. It's not worth it."

Barnes looked down at the drink like a long-lost lover he'd suddenly rekindled the flame with. *"This?"* An incredulous laugh escaped his mouth. "This, my dear, is definitely a worthy candidate for relapsing. Oh yes,

I'd say lucid hallucinations that make you question the very nature of your own sanity are right up there with the best triggers."

"What..." She stopped herself, as if posing certain questions would open doors that could never be shut again. "What did you see out there? Exactly?"

He stared directly into her eyes but didn't speak. Just when she thought he wouldn't, that he'd keep the secrets of the field all to himself, he reached inside his jacket's inner pocket and pulled out a plastic bag. She recognized the biohazard symbols at once. He slapped the bag down on the table and slid it in front of her.

"What's written on this?" he asked. When she didn't answer, he followed up with, "Anything? Any words at all?"

She swallowed. Peering down at the small ribbon of paper, the same words were printed there that had been a couple hours ago. "It says..." She turned her head, the thought of speaking the words aloud causing her gag reflex to trigger. Just seeing them filled her with deep disgust, a sickening feeling that felt like poison lining the bottom of her stomach. She wanted that feeling out of her, and she debated running to the bathroom, sticking her finger down her throat, and vomiting until every single drop came out. "It says... *touch it.*"

Barnes seemed generally surprised by this, as if maybe he were expecting her to say nothing had been scribbled there. As if he had expected something else completely. *"Touch it?"* He shrugged, the words meaning nothing to him. And they wouldn't. "I'm guessing that holds some significance to you. Something that may have happened to you at some point in your life. Something bad."

She nodded, was unable to hide the tears forming in the corners of her eyes.

"Guess it's something harrowing? Something deeply personal? Traumatic, even?"

"Yes. All of those things."

"Hm. Well, Amanda Guerrero, mine doesn't say *touch it.*"

"Yours?" She didn't understand. "Barnes, did you find another piece of paper?" She was under the impression there was only one, and, since she hadn't been apart from Barnes and Phelps for longer than five minutes that afternoon, she found it highly unlikely someone had found another clue.

He shook his head. "Same paper. Only, when I look at it, I don't see *touch it.* I see something completely different."

"What then?"

He cracked a smile; although, Amanda knew it was a front. A facade. A strong attempt at holding everything together. "A few years back, I lost someone very special to me."

She shifted uncomfortably in her seat, unable to find a position that she could stay in for very long. She couldn't blame the stool for the gift of stiffness it gave her back; her inability to secure comfort was a direct result of their conversation.

"It was before I started working at the CDC," he continued, playing with his napkin, tearing it into tiny little balls. Something Amanda used to do when she was younger to pass the time at restaurants, something that drove her parents absolutely nuts. "It was a great relationship. We connected on every level. We were planning to get hitched one day. Had it all figured out. How we'd do it. How we were going to tell our folks." He stopped, paused briefly, smiling at the memories. "Then, one day we got into a bad argument. A real nasty one. I suppose all couples have them. It's part of life, right? Anyway, there was shouting. Screaming. We both said things we didn't mean. Name-calling. Insults you say just because you want the other person to hurt. It was terrible and I'm deeply ashamed." He took a sip from his drink, allowing the taste to linger before continuing. "In the year plus we'd been together, this was our first fight. Our first *real* fight. I was sober at the time, had been for two years, so alcohol wasn't a factor and was definitely not the cause of it. Honestly, I don't even *remember* the initial cause of it. I feel like it was something mundane that just got blown out of proportion and then someone said something nasty, and it snowballed out of control from there. Is it weird that I can't remember what started it?"

Amanda chose to stay silent. She lowered her eyes to the untouched drink before her.

"Anyway. We fought. He left. *Brian.* Brian left and he..." His smile faded, the memories finally getting the best of him, tearing down that good-natured front he'd donned so well. Blinking away tears, he covered his mouth with his hands, stalling, delaying the rest of the story.

Amanda put a comforting hand on his back.

"Brian left, and he... he was in recovery too—it's how we met actually, in recovery, at a meeting—and he decided he was going to use that fight to trash his sobriety. I guess it was a way to get back at me. So, he went to the bar and got shit-faced. At least, that's what the toxicology report stated."

"He died?"

Barnes nodded.

"Car accident? Overdose?"

"Nope." Barnes shook his head, the memories continuing to drive tears down his face. "No, I feel like that would have been preferable over what actually happened, though."

Amanda felt her throat seize.

"He didn't drive that night. Didn't overdo it with the drinks, though, he did put back quite a few in a short span. He was shit-faced, sure, but he didn't drink enough to kill himself. No, Brian's downfall was that he decided to walk home from the bar instead of calling a cab, and found himself in a neighborhood he shouldn't have been in in the first place—I have no idea what he was thinking, but he was drunk, and I guess that contributed to his thinking, or lack thereof. Anyway, a couple eyewitnesses saw him talking to some guys at the bar—flirting with them—which seemed to piss off a certain section of the establishment's clientele, a few ruffians who weren't very accepting of Brian's behavior. And I don't know why or who because the police were unable to apprehend the bastards."

"Christ, Barnes."

"They followed him. Chased him most likely, again, according to the autopsy. His body was found in a local park, near the restrooms. He'd been beaten beyond recognition. His face was so swollen you couldn't even tell he had eyes. Looked like a pufferfish, ballooned so tightly his skin actually split in places. They said his lungs filled with his own blood, and technically, the cause of death was drowning. There was severe head trauma, his brain was badly bruised. If he hadn't drowned in his own blood, he probably would have been a vegetable for the rest of his life. It's likely he passed out before he died, so I guess I can take comfort in that."

A gang of tears leaked steadily from his eyes.

Amanda turned her head, disgusted.

"And the bastards," Barnes continued, his voice straining through the words, "the fuckers who killed him for no other reason than being different, took a knife and carved three letters into his neck." He tapped the biohazard bag, his finger resting on the white ribbon inside. *"F-A-G."*

Amanda had trouble swallowing. "Jesus Christ, Barnes. That's one of the most horrific things I've ever heard. I'm..." A wave of sadness tripped her up, made her temporarily lose her words. "I'm so goddamn sorry that happened to you."

He didn't react. Just stared down at the word written on the paper, the three letters left for him, *only him.* "I bet it would say something different for everyone."

"Kim Charon claims it's blank. She's pointed it out several times already."

"Well, either she's lying or whatever put this in the back of Renteria's throat meant to send *us* a message, and not her. Now that I mention it, it does feel like it's fucking with us more so than Kim and her lawyers."

"I still feel like she knows more than she's letting on."

"Same."

There was a brief pause while the two of them stared at the bar top, got lost in the shiny coating that displayed their dark reflections.

"How is any of this possible?"

"You saw what happened in the field, Amanda. I don't think we're dealing with things that are *possible.* I think we're dealing with something that's beyond our comprehension of reality."

"What did you see? Out there, in the field?"

His eyes darted. Then he squinted as if it was hard to remember, as if the details were parts of a dream and, as time dragged on, the aspects of the sequence grew murkier and murkier.

"I saw... I saw *him.* Brian. Or at least something that looked like Brian. He was off. It's hard to describe, but his arms were longer. Bent awkwardly. Uneven. His flesh was loose, like a baggy pair of jeans."

"Misshapen head?"

"Yes."

"Like something imitating what a person should look like, as though they didn't have enough information to go on."

"Yeah, like that. Like a sculpture and the artist had only seen the subject a handful of times and went off its memory. Or maybe not at all. Like the artist had only *heard* what the subject looked like and had never actually seen it."

Amanda felt herself trembling. She looked down at her hand, found it shaking against the bar top. A cold, hollow sensation rummaged through her. Her skin was hard, and the back of her neck tingled, icy fingers dancing across her flesh. "What the hell was that thing, Barnes? What does *'everything is sixty-nine'* mean?"

"I don't know. But I think we should find out."

She nodded. He didn't delve into the quandary of *sixty-nine* and what that number could possibly mean to the thing in the field, but Amanda knew Barnes had heard it speak those same words. *Everything is sixty-nine.* She could see it in his eyes. The field had given him a similar experience—maybe not the same exact one, but something close.

Whatever the thing was, it could clearly see inside their heads, the stuff that was buried there.

"I think we should too."

Barnes had stopped the tears. A smile somehow found its way onto his face, and he even let out a small laugh. "Got a text from Cohen on the way here. Plane emergency landed in Baltimore. Something with the landing gear. Everyone's safe, but you have to wonder."

Amanda nodded, already knowing the scoop. Cohen had texted her when he had landed at Baltimore-Washington International a half hour ago. *"Sixty-nine."*

"Yep. Sixty-fucking-nine."

Her eyes fell to his drink. "Wish you hadn't destroyed your sobriety, Barnes. Goddamn you."

Casually, he slid the glass in front of her. "Go ahead. Have a sip."

She didn't at first, but his eyes insisted.

"Go ahead," he encouraged. "One sip."

She did. It tasted like Cherry Coke sans a single drop of alcohol.

His smile broadened. "If I didn't drink when someone murdered my boyfriend, my future husband, in cold blood, then I'm sure as fuck not going to let whatever's happening at Spring Lakes break me."

She threw herself at him, wrapping her arms around his shoulders, squeezing him as if she never meant to let go.

He hugged her back.

They stayed that way and cried into each other's shoulders for a few minutes before paying their tab. Before heading back to Spring Lakes. Where all hell was threatening to break loose.

13

NO ONE ENJOYED the look that had sprouted on Kim Charon's face, not even her two lawyers. They were back in her office, telling her their plan, their reasons behind heading back into the woods, and the woman wasn't having any of it.

"Maybe I'm not following," Kim said, curling her upper lip. "You want to head back into the woods because you think there's a man out there, and that he is responsible for the sixty-niners—your word—and their current medical condition?"

Barnes reacted first. "I think we're beyond a logical medical diagnosis. Whatever equipment our co-workers are eventually going to bring, if and when they get here, isn't going to tell us shit."

Kim looked as if he'd slapped her.

Before she could respond, Amanda opened her mouth. "What Barnes is trying to say, is that we've all seen the evidence. The video, the mysterious piece of paper that came out of Mr. Renteria's mouth."

"The one that's blank? That could have been staged there?" Kim leaned back and folded her arms, turned her head to the side and sighed dramatically. "This is getting tiresome, Mrs. Guerrero."

"I understand that, I really do. But that piece of paper... well, it wasn't blank. Not for us." She motioned to Barnes and Phelps. "We all saw something written there, something meaningful to us. Something that brought back a painful memory. I don't know why the paper was blank to you and your lawyers. I don't know why we are the only ones who can see it. But I can assure you the answers are out there, in the field."

Kim wasn't buying it. She only stared at them, a feral look capturing her eyes.

"We're not lying to you," Amanda added. "We're not trying to deceive you. We're telling the truth. Whatever is happening in your facility..."

"Is what? Supernatural? Is that what you're telling me?"

Amanda shook her head. "No, I don't know. We don't know that, not for certain. But there is *something* out there in the woods. Something..."

Awful. Heinous. Something evil. Something that existed long before man, something that would live on long after our existence.

She cleared her throat. "Whatever is out there," Amanda said, tapping the table with her finger, "is responsible for what we've seen here today."

"It told us *'everything is sixty-nine',"* Phelps said, speaking for what felt like the first time since their return from the woods. "It actually told us that."

"And what the hell does that mean? It *told* you that?" Kim's face wrinkled in several unflattering places. Her eyes were wide, stretched to their limit. "How does a field tell you things?"

"There was a man out there," Amanda said. "At least we think he was a man. It's possible it was just an illusion, the field projecting an image to make us... to make *it* seem more... *acceptable. More real."*

Kim leaned forward and folded her hands on the table. "What the hell are you people talking about? This is lunacy. Have you all lost your goddamn minds?"

"I know it sounds nuts—hell, it sounds nuts to us and we've experienced it. But the field—"

"The field that doesn't exist? The one you can't find anymore?"

Amanda watched Hatterman and Hart turn sideways, cup their hands over their mouths, concealing their cynical smiles.

Barnes laughed. "Because it didn't want to be found."

Now the woman turned her head, stared at him, as if he'd offended her in some way.

"Because we had the cops with us. I'm sure of that now. There was no way we could have gotten turned around. No, for whatever reason, it didn't want to be found. It... it tricked us."

"The field tricked you?" Now Kim wore a big smile. Her eyes were still stretched with amazement, but it was the smile that really wrenched Amanda's nerves. The woman was less pissed off about their failures and more entertained by the story they'd come up with. "Let me get this straight—the field has the power to make you see whatever it wants? It can just... disappear? Poof. Like that?"

Yes, it can, Amanda wanted to respond, but she couldn't find the courage to speak those words aloud. Admitting the thing had that much ability, that much influence over reality, frightened her to no end.

"What other magical powers does this field have?" Kim rested her chin in her hands, pretending she actually cared what they were going to say. When they didn't answer, realizing she was playing with them now, having a little fun for her troubles, she reached into her desk drawer and retrieved a small phonebook. "Tell you what. I can call the local psychiatric facility and tell them the three of you will be dropping by. I'm sure they'd love to hear all about this magical field."

Amanda reached out, put her hand over Kim's, preventing her from opening the book. "You don't have to make any phone calls. We'll leave if that's what you want. We'll go peacefully, without protest. You'll never hear from us ever again."

"What I want is for you three to figure out exactly what *the fuck* is happening to my clients. It's been over three hours and you haven't produced a single goddamn thing that makes any fucking sense. Not even a plausible guess."

"I told you I thought the disease was neurological."

"That was before you started blathering about magical fields and scary woodland creatures."

"I never used the word 'creature', okay?"

Kim squinted. "Listen to me and listen to me goddamn good. If you don't get your shit together and do your goddamn jobs, not only am I going to make it my life's mission to see you three fired from the CDC, but I'm also going to press charges."

"Charges for what exactly?" Barnes asked calmly. He seemed more amused than confrontational.

"For... endangering our clients and the people who work here. You might even see me in court after all of this is over."

Her lawyers perked up, suddenly gathering themselves and standing still, displaying the professionalism they hadn't shown since Amanda had started talking about the field and whatever might be metaphysically stalking the grounds of Spring Lakes.

Barnes, rolling his eyes, stood up. "Listen to me now, you callous cunt." Kim recoiled as if he'd thrown a punch. Her mouth dropped open. Before she could utter a response, Barnes continued. "We've done nothing but try to help since we've arrived. This, this *sixty-nine* business is beyond us. Okay? It's beyond any rational explanation, any scientific analysis. What you have out there is a whole new ballgame. Something this world has never seen before, and it cannot be explained through numbers and reports and results pulled from a fucking lab. There aren't any cures, no vaccines, nothing. There is—"

"We don't actually know that yet," Phelps said, cutting him off. "It's possible that we could have overlooked this whole thing. Could be a virus. We might not have found it because we don't know what antibodies to look for."

Silence descended on the room like a plague.

"Finally," Kim said after it was time for the awkward break to end. "Finally, someone says something sensible."

"We might have been so thrown off by the blood work, how all the results were aligned, that we didn't even consider a viral sickness."

"No one else has..." Amanda started but trailed off when she saw the way Phelps was staring at her. She shot her a quick *shut-the-hell-up* glance. Phelps's eyes narrowed subtly, making sure not to give Kim any ideas. Amanda turned her own gaze back on the woman behind the desk. "I mean, we could always look into that, even if that seems entirely unlikely."

Kim agreed, nodding vigorously. "I think that's a swell idea. Now, why don't the three of you get to work? You've wasted enough of my time already."

14

"**S**HE'S NOT GOING to help us," Barnes said, smoking, taking long drags from his borrowed cigarette. "We're on our own."

"It's almost better that way," Amanda said, gazing at the entrance into the woods, the narrow path that hardly looked like one unless you were right next to it. She knew her mind had been altered by her experience inside the woods, but she thought she heard someone whispering in her ear. Someone calling to her from a distance. She did her best to block out the faint white noise, the constant chatter of some unknown identity. "We wouldn't want anyone else ending up like Cunningham, would we?"

"That bitch maybe," Barnes said, smiling behind a thin veil of smoke, jerking his thumb toward Kim's office.

She was jealous that Barnes had gotten to call her a "cunt" before she could. Still, it had been satisfying all the same. Amanda couldn't help but smirk when she recalled the woman's reaction, how she jumped in her seat. "In all seriousness, I think it's better if we go it alone. I think... I get the sense that's what *it* wants. I mean, no one else can see what's written on the paper except for us."

"Unless they're lying," Phelps added.

"Right. There's that."

"Can we talk about *it* for a moment?" Phelps's cigarette dangled from the corner of her mouth, plumes of smoke shrouding the air in front of her. "What do you guys think it is?"

Barnes shook his head. "I have no idea. But did you feel weird when we got close to it? There was this sense... this presence."

"I felt it, too," Amanda said, her mouth going dry the second she thought about that moment, the confrontation in the field. Standing before the thing as it poorly imitated her grandfather, the way her skin rippled with gooseflesh. "It was like, whatever it was, had gotten inside my brain. I could feel it rooting around in there. Probing. Digging up the past as if it were literally something buried in a field. Digging deep. Unearthing all these things. Drawing it out of the darkness."

Barnes nodded. "Yep. Pretty much how I felt. Like it had violated my memories, accessed my brain and turned my thoughts into its weapon. And you know what? It fucking worked." He shivered despite the warm conditions, the summery way the sun touched their skin.

Phelps also caught a case of the chills. "It's fucking evil, whatever it is."

Amanda couldn't disagree. She'd felt the thing from the field inside her, rummaging around her memories, consuming them like... like...

The idea hit her, fast and suddenly, and when the notion fully formed, she almost screamed.

"Guys," she said, turning toward the door. "What if it's, whatever *it* is, let's just call it The Field—what if The Field is inside the sixty-niners?"

"How do you mean?" Barnes asked, casting his cigarette into the parking lot. "Inside them how?"

Amanda faced Spring Lakes' entrance, staring down the empty hall. "What if it's using them for something. Like, feeding off their minds. Drawing things from us. Using them to get to us."

Phelps paced the handicap ramp. "How does that make sense?"

Amanda shrugged. "The paper. The notes to us. It came from them. Well, it came from Mr. Renteria. Then Mrs. Finch. She was out there. In the field. Praying to it. Wasn't she? That's what she was doing, I think."

A moment passed, the idea of the woman kneeling before The Field, praying to it, filled their thoughts, polluted their minds, and crowded them with an undeniable terror, the kind that runs through the bloodstream, infecting all parts of the body with a cold numbing sensation, one that makes you check to see if your body is still intact.

Amanda twisted toward them. "We have to stop it. The Field. We have to head back there and figure out what it wants, how to stop it." She breathed slowly, her heart racing along with her thoughts. "We stop The Field, we help *them*," she added, nodding toward the facility and the victims within.

"But how do we stop *it*?" Barnes asked. "How do you stop something that... that *isn't?* That isn't a real thing. That has the power to use our memories against us?"

"I have no idea. But like finding the cure to any disease," she said, turning to the door and taking the first step inside, "we have to experiment."

● ● ●

Amanda sat across from one of the sixty-niners; a woman named Helen Grace. She was frozen with her back arched forward, looking over a deck of cards spread out in a game of Solitaire. Her stare was focused on the game, one hand holding the two of clubs, while the other had been placed on the table, using her arm to support the rest of her body. Her face had been fixed in a startled expression, as if she'd felt whatever had infiltrated her before it had taken over and was completely confused by the sudden intrusion. The way her lips were pursed suggested she might have felt some pain before going stiff.

Amanda shone the light in her eyes and gauged their reaction. The brightness did nothing to move them, and the woman remained in her ever-still pose.

Phelps wrapped an inflatable cuff around the woman's arm and took her blood pressure.

"Normal?" Amanda asked.

She nodded. "One-twenty over eighty. Precise."

Amanda didn't exactly like that reading—it was too perfect. Like the thing that had frozen her knew what the perfect score was and had made it so. Just like the blood work. "All right. When Renteria moved, what were we doing?"

Barnes stepped next to Helen, directing his flashlight into the sixty-nine-year-old's right ear. "We tampered with him."

"That's right. We were testing his brain, stimulating him, seeing how he interacted when we introduced electrical impulses."

"Do you think it's an electrical thing?" asked Phelps.

"I have no idea. But I'd like to introduce this." She held up a syringe loaded with clear fluid.

"Is that a flu shot?"

"Yes. Yes, that's exactly what it is."

"And what do you think that'll do?"

Barnes clicked off his flashlight. "She's hoping that introducing a live strain of something, a foreign antibody, will affect this woman's body the same as when we fucked with Renteria's brainwaves." Barnes flashed a knowing smile. "Am I right?"

Amanda snapped her fingers. "You got it. Who wants to do the honors?"

There were no takers.

"All right, guess I'm doing this myself."

Phelps began to pace back and forth. "Not so sure I'm on board with this."

"What's not to like?" She dipped the needle into the old woman's arm and emptied the vaccine into her vein.

Once finished, she retracted the needle and threw away the syringe in the garbage.

They waited.

For five minutes.

They studied the woman. Phelps continued to monitor her blood pressure while Barnes continued to look inside her ears, nose, and throat. Neither reported any significant changes; in fact, there were no changes at all. Helen Grace continued to look normal, despite the fact she was paralyzed, unable to move a single muscle.

"How long do we wait?" Phelps asked.

"A few more minutes," Amanda answered. "Let it work."

"A flu shot could take hours to register," Barnes said. "Takes weeks to become effective."

Amanda wagged her finger. "It'll take weeks for antibodies to form, sure, but we're not trying to protect Mrs. Grace from the fucking flu—we're trying to see what happens when her immune system responds to a foreign substance. That should be almost instant."

Phelps nodded. "If this thing is controlling her body..."

Barnes's eyes lit up. "Then it's in control of her immune system too."

"It's why I think it reacted when we sent the electrical pulses into Renteria's brain. It doesn't want to be disturbed. The system will fight off any interference."

"Like the field."

Amanda closed her eyes, nodded. "Like the fucking field."

"None of this explains sixty-nine," Phelps said. "Why is it only affecting those sixty-nine years of age? There has to be a reason for it."

Amanda shrugged. "Maybe because the number holds some significance to this thing. It's important to it. There's meaning behind the number, to The Field anyway. For whatever reason, it selected them." Amanda noticed Barnes and Phelps staring at her. "Just a guess, I mean."

Yes, it was a guess, but it seemed like she knew things. And how did she know them? She had no clue. In the back of her mind, she wondered if stumbling upon the field, letting it *touch* her, had something to do with the knowledge. The idea showered her with chills. Her spine danced as the prickly, cold sensation ran down it.

They waited some more. Nothing happened. The woman continued to stay frozen, looking down at the card game she might never finish, her eyes glued to the table. Amanda pitied her, felt bad about being able to do nothing to help her. To save her. Ultimately the woman would probably die here, like this, incapacitated for all eternity. She wondered what it was going to take to remove them from the premises, the sixty-niners, what kind of machinery it would take to lift them. If several nurses and security guards couldn't get it done, what would it take?

Feels like they're full of lead, Amanda had read in one of the statements they'd made everyone fill out. *Weighed as much as an elephant and then some.*

She shook her head. It was no use thinking about these things now, not when there was still more work to do. More experiments to conduct, more tests to run. She'd run them all until she got the thing to wake again, to react to something. She wanted to see how it behaved when prodded. The thought of riling up this thing, rousing it from whatever dream-filled world it currently inhabited, filled her with a sense of peace. She wanted nothing more than to ruffle its feathers. Dig under its skin as it had dug into her mind, messed around in there.

Evil, Phelps had called it. Amanda couldn't disagree, not after it had shown her those things in the field, not when it had come to her under the guise of the vilest human being she'd ever encountered.

(touch it)

(go ahead, it's fun)

(it's a game)

(you like games, don't you)

(touch it, tug it)

She needed more coffee. Standing up, she took a deep breath, and looked at Helen Grace one last time, hoping to see the slightest difference in her stature. But there was none. The expressionless masks worn on her employees' faces told her that.

"What do you want us to do, boss?" Barnes asked.

She put her hands on her hips, surveyed the small living quarters. She checked the door to see if Kim Charon and her two lapdogs were pacing the hallway, listening in on their conversations, trying to squirrel away all the information they could for later, when it was time to file their lawsuit against the CDC. That was what it would come down to, Amanda was sure of it. "I'd say raid the van for more vaccines. I'd like to introduce as many outside influences as possible. Something live, maybe."

Phelps perked up. "I think I have a measles vaccination in the van."

Amanda snapped her fingers. "Perfect. Grab it and let's—"

Helen lifted her head back from the card game and her spine straightened out, a fluid, yet somewhat robotic movement that caused all three of them to back away. Her entire body began shaking, quivering as if she'd stepped out of a hot shower and into a freezer. Her head twitched, snapping in different directions. Eyes rolling back, Helen opened her mouth and let go of an inhuman cry, something that sounded off like a foghorn.

The three CDC employees jumped back, covering their ears. When the sound stopped—after ten long seconds—they rushed forward, coming to the woman's side. Still shaking involuntarily, she flung out her hand, striking Phelps across the chest with enough force to knock her off her feet. She fell to the ground, her head slamming against the dorm's carpeted floor. The cushiony surface saved her from serious injury, but she was still slow to react. Barnes immediately went to her aid while Amanda concentrated on the woman.

Helen stood, her body continuing to quake. She'd seemed to gain control over her head because it stopped trembling, and, instead, it moved back and forth at odd angles, smoothly. As if someone who'd never had control over the muscles and nerves in their neck might look around.

The sight of Helen Grace, her inhuman white eyes, was enough to drive Amanda back to the far wall. She stood there, quivering with fear, as the thing tried to walk toward her. Awkwardly, the legs moved, its toes bending inward like an infant attempting its first steps. It made for her, but then fell flat on its face.

The thought of stepping on the back Helen Grace's head, crushing her skull and the thing that had laid claim to her brain, was strong. She pictured herself doing it, ending the woman's life right then and there, but then thought about how crazy that was. How she'd never convince a jury of what had happened at Spring Lakes.

An earthly smell permeated the air, a wet-dirt perfume that seemed to emanate from Helen's body.

Amanda kept against the wall, watching the thing from the field pick itself off the floor. It failed, unable to coordinate such a maneuver, and, instead of doing so, it picked up Helen's head, directing its milky eyes at Amanda.

"*Fu-ool,*" it rasped, sounding like a bucket of rattlesnakes. "*Fu-ind me. Fu-ind me. Juh-oin me. I ue-eet. You-eer. Druh-eams.*"

Amanda couldn't stop herself. She lashed out, kicking the woman across her face. The kick, one she hadn't used since she was eight and had loved to play soccer, landed flush. The impact drove the woman's head sideways, and she heard a loud crack rip through the room. Her first thought was that she'd broken the woman's neck. Images of a women's prison suddenly came forth, *Orange is the New Black* minus all the cute laughs and life lessons and dramatic storylines. Just pure hell. That was what she was thinking when Helen swung her head back toward her, those white eyes almost glowing in the dim light of the room.

The lights flickered, the bulb buzzing behind the lampshade, threatening them with more darkness.

The thing inside Helen howled with laughter, a barbaric noise that grated on Amanda's ears.

"*Fu-ool. Fu-ool. Fuuuuuuuu-oooooooool.*"

And then Helen's head fell to the carpet, the white veil in her eyes shrinking, retreating to wherever it had come from. The lights stopped flickering. That fusty odor died at once. The room stood still, along with the entire world. No one breathed.

Barnes and Phelps looked up at Amanda from the floor. She finally took a breath, gasped for fresh air. She was unable to speak.

Down the hall, they heard footsteps. Fast. As if a herd was galloping toward them. A thunderous collection of feet stampeding the carpet.

And then, someone, Kim, she discovered, asked, "*What the hell is going on in there?*"

15

PHELPS WAS A researcher. She couldn't help it; it was in her blood. She'd come from a long line of academic scholars, doctors and professors. Her mother had gone to Yale, where she'd met her father, and the two had gone on to work for private organizations in the medical field, working on cancer research, as well as other deadly diseases. Phelps's path led her to the CDC, where she'd been working for two years now, straight out of college. Research had been a part of her life for as long as she could read and write. School had always been her top priority, taking precedence over things like family and friends. She never had much in the way of friends, a few study buddies that had come and gone over the years. *Research* had always been (and always would be) her BFF.

Phelps found herself scouring the Internet in a cramped back office. Under ordinary circumstances she might have headed down to the local library, conducted her research there in the blissful silence, the smell of old, worn books always adding to the rush of a good study session, but there was no time for that. The computer in the back office was all she had now, and Amanda and Barnes had decided it was probably best if they left for The Field within the hour. Which left her little time to dig into a few relevant topics.

Sixty-nine.

"What are you looking for?" Amanda had asked when Phelps had first settled in back there, sat down with a giant cup of Starbucks and began her work. "What do you think you'll find?"

"We need to figure out what we're dealing with," she had told her. "If we go back to The Field without any knowledge of who or what is out there, our chances of defeating it—if that's what we plan to do—are zero."

Amanda had told her she was right, that it was impossible to conquer something that they knew virtually nothing about, though, she had also expressed her doubt in the Internet and its ability to inform them of whatever existed out there beyond the trees. And, although, she had offered no other advice in the way of where to start, she had patted Phelps on the shoulder, and told her to hurry up because time was short and she didn't know how much longer they had until Kim would flip and attempt to shut this whole thing down. She'd left her to it after that, headed back out into the hall to make her rounds and check on the sixty-niners, and to, hopefully, quell the growing doubt that resided within their not-so-hospitable host.

So, Phelps did what she'd always done best and combed the Internet for information, shuffling through countless pages of research. She started small, typing things like "LONG TERM PARALYSIS" along with the other symptoms their patients were exhibiting and came up pretty empty. There was nothing on the Internet that explained what was happening at Spring Lakes, but it wasn't like she had expected to find another case of it out there. She'd have heard of it, or, at the very least, Amanda would have. But still, it was worth investing five minutes, hoping somebody out there had experienced a similar event. Nothing came up, so she moved on to the next topic of interest.

The number.

Sixty-nine.

She keyed in "The significance of 69" and the search engine pulled 207 million results. After training her mind to skip all the dirty stuff, she came across a few tidbits that weren't very useful, but stuff that was interesting. 69, on some new age spiritualist's numerology site, meant quite a few things, some of which resonated—it was said to be connected with family, health, happiness, and compassion. If you kept seeing the number sixty-nine in your life, that meant good things were to come. Phelps got a laugh out of that, considering where the number had brought her and her team, and immediately closed the page, taking her research elsewhere. She scanned through message boards frequented by those who claimed to have seen the number everywhere, and what it could possibly mean in the scope of the great universe. There were hundreds of replies, some of them offering messages of encouragement, telling the original poster that something good awaited them on the horizon, that the yin-and-yang parallel of the number signified some great cosmic shift and fortunes were headed their way. Others chimed in to tell the poster she was probably horny and needed some action, that pent-up sexual frustration was her reason for seeing the number everywhere.

After about twenty minutes of clicking through blog posts and message boards, Phelps leaned back in her seat, took off her glasses and rubbed her eyes. She stretched, put her glasses back on, took a few sips of her cooling coffee, and went back to work.

Sixty-nine wasn't getting her anywhere, though she did find the bits about the symmetrical aspects of the number interesting. Like the symbols from most major religions (crosses, stars, moons), sixty-nine was similar in that regard. There was power in symmetry, some believed, a magic bond between the sequence and the unearthly realm beyond our own comprehension.

Next, she scouted the local history, researching the area around Spring Lake, New Jersey. She searched for strange sightings in the neighborhood, even the surrounding towns, keeping an eye out for any peculiar happenings, especially in wooded areas. One whacko had written a blog dedicated to the Jersey Devil and claimed to have seen sightings all throughout the state, including one in Spring Lake, five miles from where the assisted living facility was located. Phelps didn't give the story much of a chance, writing it off as fiction almost immediately, and although the Jersey Devil being their culprit made a grand story, it wasn't one she'd explore. Though, The Field had given off *devilish* vibes.

This is a devil of a different sort, she thought, closing the page.

Phelps wasn't a believer of religious ideologies, theories on heaven or hell, even though she found the topic interesting and found it made for good conversation especially since she'd always taken the scientific approach to life's most popular unanswered questions. But even she could admit there were things out there that science couldn't fully explain. That there were gaps between what could be proven and what could not.

Like, The Field.

Yes, like that. A field that had shown her things, things she was pretty sure she'd buried deep inside the catacombs of her mind.

A cold sensation tickled the back of her neck when she thought back to what she'd seen out there moving among the trees.

(our secret)

No, don't think about it. Thinking about it gives the thing power. It wants us to visit the past. Live there.

She'd overheard Barnes and Amanda talking about the paper they'd found in Renteria's throat, said it had shown them different words. When it had been her turn to peek, her heart nearly stopped. She didn't dare let her eyes linger over the words.

(our secret)

(tell no one)

(cough-cough)

(trust you)

She couldn't keep out the thoughts. The tight office faded, giving way to that hospital room. Her grandmother lay on the bed, struggling for breath. They'd already excised one lung and were fixing to take thirty-three percent of the second, where the cancer had grabbed hold and refused to let go. Phelps's parents were still debating whether to put the eighty-two-year-old through the process again; in fact, they'd gone off to the cafeteria to discuss exactly that. Left Phelps alone with the old woman, to watch over her, to keep her company. She hadn't felt uncomfortable with the task until she had woken up.

And started talking.

"Hey, Grandmother," she said, brushing white curls of hair off her forehead. "How are you feeling?"

Her grandmother smiled. "Fine, sweetheart. Just fine." She coughed, a chest-rattling outburst that caused immediate concern. Phelps supposed the cough was normal, normal for *her,* but still—the way her chest crackled sped up Phelps's heart rate.

"What were you dreaming about?" Phelps asked her, funny because when she was a little girl and woke up from naps, her grandmother would always ask her that very question.

"Oh, the boys again. Always the boys."

Phelps smiled this time, thinking of her father and her uncle, what they must have been like when they were younger. The stories she'd heard. "Pop and Uncle Marty must have been quite the handful."

Grandmother grinned, and for some reason, the way her lips spread apart sent a chill down Phelps's back. "No, not them. Not *my* boys. *The other boys.*"

Immediately, Phelps felt uneasy. Invisible spiders crawled across her shoulders. She had no idea what the old woman was talking about, but the tone of her voice warned her—whatever it was, she didn't want to hear it.

"Oh, okay. Well, that's nice, Grandmother. Can I get you something to eat? I think I have—"

"Do you know what boys I'm talking about?"

Phelps looked away, her eyes focused on her jacket and the breakfast bar she'd brought with her. She felt her grandmother's eyes probing her, studying her, peering through her, into her soul. Phelps checked her phone, hoping someone would call, hoping someone would relieve her of this troubling situation.

But she had no one. No friends. No college boyfriends. She wasn't close with her cousins, aunts and uncles. They all lived far away and rarely talked to her. Never even bothered to call and wish her a happy birthday or a Merry Christmas.

No one.

No one loves you.

(the boys)

"No, grandmother," she said, knowing she shouldn't feed whatever monster her grandmother had placed between them. It was the way she had said *the boys* that freaked her out, for no other reason than the tone of her voice. Oh, and that grin didn't help. She was old, eighty-two now, but she didn't have dementia, had never once exhibited Alzheimer's symptoms. She'd always been lucid, though, after her husband died a few years back, she had gotten a little zanier. But nothing terrible. Nothing like the grin she now wore, the crack between her lips that displayed semi-decayed teeth, blackening near the gum-lines. "No, I don't."

"We killed them," she said, dead serious. She wasn't grinning anymore. She glared directly at Phelps—no, not *at* her. Past her.

Phelps turned, saw nothing but the sink and the mirror. Her grandmother was looking into the mirror as if she were telling the story to herself.

"Arthur and me. We killed them. They never knew. Never found out. We took them, walking home from school. Only one each year to avoid suspicion. Brought them home." Her eyes turned on her granddaughter. Phelps felt tears rolling down her cheeks. She knew her grandmother wasn't making this up, wasn't joking. She never joked, not like this. At first, she thought the woman had just lost it—her mind had finally cracked under the stress of the doctor's visits, the chemotherapy, the surgeries. But something in her eyes, that little twinkle, gave away what this truly was—a *confession*. "Brought them home and diced them up into pieces. Ate what we could. We were terrible at first. Hardly any meat. Hardly any—"

"Stop," Phelps said, getting up and rushing over to the sink. Her vomit covered the white porcelain, every inch. When done, she wiped her mouth on a paper towel, tossed it into the garbage. "Stop."

She was in the field now. In the middle of the clearing, in the center of the trampled tall grass. It was night. The stars speckled the dark skies. Next to her rested grandmother's hospital bed, the old woman comfortably tucked under the covers. Peering at her. Into her. Probing her thoughts.

"I know you hate me, child." The voice came out in a rasp. She didn't remember her grandmother's voice ever being that deep, but, then again, this wasn't her. An imitation, The Field's best. "I know you hate me for what I've done. I won't apologize for it. It was good. I liked killing those boys. Arthur did, too."

Phelps dropped to her knees. Tears ran freely from her eyes; there was nothing she could do to stop them.

"You want to know why we never took you? Or your brother?" The old woman laughed with delight.

"You were our family, sweetie. We loved you. The both of you. We'd never do anything to hurt you. No, no, no. You were always safe with us. It was the boys we liked. The nameless boys. The faceless boys. We never read the papers, never followed up on their strange disappearances. Once a year we'd take them, careful so no one would suspect. Never the same town twice. It was our Christmas present to ourselves. Oh, Merry Christmas, dear."

Her face warped into some melted-wax mask, as if the thing imitating her suddenly wanted to purge its human qualities—all monster from here on out. The thing's teeth grew sharp and long, ivory stalactites in the thing's cavernous mouth. Blood sputtered over its lips, blood and other unknown fluids, dark like the sky above them. She still smelled the hospital, the faint odor of potent antiseptics and bleach. There were new smells now, overriding the old. Alien scents. Fruity, yet, unique. They choked the air around her, seeped into *her*, and she couldn't look away from the awful sight of the thing her grandmother had become, which was fitting because that was much like how she had viewed her after the hospital confession—a repulsive monster.

She was glad the woman had died a horrible, painful, and long death.

(our secret)
(tell no one)
(the boys)
(once a year)

She was back in the office, the walls seeming closer than they ever were. On the monitor, several news articles had populated, each of them dating back to the seventies and eighties, even the nineties. They all took place in central Kentucky, Phelps's home state. Near the town where her grandparents had lived. Each article showed their faces, displayed their names. Names and faces of the missing little boys who were never found.

Names and faces that haunted Phelps's dreams from time to time. Names and faces that begged for her help, begged for their missing bodies to be found, reunited with their mothers and fathers, once and for all. Begging her to assist in their unsolved murders.

They came to her in dreams. Nightmares. And they'd never leave. She knew that. Not as long as she held onto her grandmother's confession. Not until she told the world what she knew.

They killed them. Twenty-five boys. They killed them and buried their bodies in the woods near their house. Never to be found.

Unless she said something to someone, told the local police. But she couldn't. Couldn't bring that down on their family. Her parents might not understand. Her *father* definitely wouldn't. Even if everything she claimed was found to be true, he'd still think of her differently. Either hold it against her for disgracing their family or hold it against her for not coming forward with the truth sooner. He was like that. He'd cut her out of his life completely either way. And she didn't want that. She had no one in her life who meant anything, save for her parents, and she couldn't risk losing them. Their love.

She needed them.

Didn't she?

Phelps looked at the clock on the computer monitor and realized she'd just lost ten minutes to that awful memory, that day at the hospital she'd trained herself to never think of again.

That thing in the field.

It had touched her, here, and brought that day back to her. Delivered her to the hungry mouth of the past. Fed her to her own secrets. Used her own brain against her. When she'd been in the field, when Cunningham had ripped out his own eyes, she had seen her grandmother, propped up on the hospital bed, grinning that sick, terrible grin. She could tell she was thinking about the boys, *her* boys, the ones she'd kidnapped with her husband, gutted in their kitchen, stripped the meat from their bones, and... and even ate a little.

She could tell she'd been thinking this because she'd been foaming at the mouth. Drooling.

She was hungry. The Field was. And Phelps's memories were the perfect snack.

● ● ●

After she hit the Keurig and refilled her coffee, Phelps cleared her mind, through a series of meditative exercises she'd learned over the last few years, and immediately got back into research mode. She started digging through the town's history, most notably the newspaper articles reporting on strange deaths. Since the "strange sightings" keyword search proved relatively pointless, she'd chosen "strange deaths" as her next best option. Scrolling through the four pages of results, she finally stopped when the headline, "SPRING LAKE WOMAN DIES SUDDENLY AND MYSTERIOUSLY" populated on the feed.

Her heart jumped as she clicked on the article.

This was what she'd hoped for.

"Holy shit," she said, popping a cigarette in her mouth. She wondered how pissed Kim Charon would be if she lit up back here. Her heart raced as she scrolled through the article, hanging onto every word. "Holy fucking shit."

Last week, a woman, Lacey Metcalf, 69, died at Spring Lakes Assisted Living. Her death was sudden. As of right now, there is no cause. Ms. Metcalf was found in her room, sitting in her rocking chair, seemingly paralyzed at first, but later pronounced dead by local medical examiner, Henry Lee, at 8:59 Tuesday morning.

Lee told reporters that it took six men to carry her out.

"Damndest thing I'd ever seen. Woman couldn't have weighed a hundred pounds soaking wet. Took six of us and we were struggling."

Lee offered no medical explanation for the woman's mysterious heaviness and a cause of death has not yet been determined.

"Natural causes would be my guess," Lee said.

Natural causes, Phelps thought. *Yeah, right.* There was nothing natural about any of this.

She opened a new search window and typed "SPRING LAKES ASSISTED LIVING DEATHS" into the new bar. She narrowed the search to include New Jersey only, as there were other Spring Lakes assisted living facilities across the country. Then she only allowed articles containing the number "69" to remain visible.

Her heart lurched.

She opened each article in a new tab.

Each article documented the strange deaths that had taken place here. Over the last thirty years, there had been eleven of them. All with the same symptoms. The deceased appearing paralyzed at first but dying within twenty-four hours. All of them weighing triple, quadruple what they should. Different medical examiners provided different quotes, but each held the same main idea—these were *strange deaths,* however, *natural* was the word they'd used in every single case.

"Holy shit," Phelps said, the unlit cigarette falling onto the desk. She jotted down the years from when the articles had been written. "Shit, shit, shit."

Half of them had happened over the last five years.

"How come no one looked into this?" she asked herself and got up to find Amanda and Barnes, until she noticed a quote on the latest article, written less than a year ago.

"We are deeply saddened by what happened here," the quote said. *"We, at Spring Lakes, will greatly miss Mr. Allen." When asked if Mr. Allen exhibited any strange behaviors or sickness of late, director Kimberly Charon simply replied, "No. None at all. This is quite a shock to all of us."*

Phelps went back through the articles, reading every word instead of skimming them for keywords. Some of them contained quotes from Charon, some didn't. The ones that didn't were absent of any official statement from the facility. Anything before ten years ago, the response from the facility had come from an Eduardo Ramirez, the director at the time. His quotes were equally uninspiring and smelled like bullshit all the same.

She read Charon's quotes again.

She knew. That bitch, she knew the whole the goddamn time.

As she ran down the hall to find Amanda and Barnes, she wondered what else Kim was hiding from them.

16

AMANDA PLOPPED THE folder full of news articles down on the desk. Kim glanced at the headlines peeking out from the top. WOMAN, 69, DIES MYSTERIOUSLY AT ASSISTED LIVING FACILITY.

Kim straightened her posture, ready to strike an intimidating pose, gave her jacket a nervous tug, and faced her three visitors, all of them wearing expressions of disgust and utter disappointment. "I don't see what this has to do with anything?"

Amanda stared sharply at the woman while Barnes and Phelps scoffed from behind her. "You lied to us."

"I did no such thing." Her lawyers shifted uncomfortably, the nature of this conversation befuddling them.

"People have died here. Eleven of them." Amanda pointed toward the door. "The same way these people are dying out there."

She watched the woman's throat bob. "Hatterman, Hart," she said to the two men. "Please excuse us. Give us a little privacy, will you?"

The shorter, portly man known as Hart raised his finger. "I must object—"

"And I must insist you leave at once."

There was no more conversation about it. The two lawyers shuffled toward the door, objecting quietly on the way out. Once they were gone, Kim told Barnes to shut the door, which he did without hesitation.

"You have to promise me that whatever is about to be said will not leave this room." The tone of Kim's voice caught Amanda off guard. She wasn't the confident, sassy woman she'd been only moments ago. Her demeanor had shifted. She was scared now, maybe. Unsure of herself. Not confident of the words that were about to be spoken.

The three remained silent, promising no such thing.

"Do I have your word?" asked Kim, almost as if she were begging. Whatever she had to say shook the woman. Scrambled her assertiveness. Amanda watched the woman's fingers tremble ever-so-slightly. When Kim noticed Amanda was staring, she covered up one hand with the other, pretended to massage the muscle between her thumb and forefinger.

"Why don't you just tell us," said Amanda, "and we'll judge as to whether this warrants anyone else knowing."

Kim sighed, realizing that was the best they could do. It wouldn't get any better than that, plus she probably figured her three visitors already had a low opinion of her. The only way to prevent them from going to the authorities, which would undoubtedly stunt her career at Spring Lakes, was to set the situation straight. Come clean. Maybe they would have mercy.

Amanda figured it'd have to be a pretty good reason for the three of them *not* to throw her under the bus.

She hid things from us. Details. Deaths of almost a dozen sixty-nine-year-olds. Granted, not all of them were under her watch, but Amanda was smart enough to know the woman was at least aware of the other deaths. She knew Kim would know the history of this place, every single thing that had transpired under its roof. *Why hadn't she told us?*

What is she hiding?

She probably figured the current situation would play out like the others. Come tomorrow, the sixty-niners would die. The CDC would investigate and find no trace of any illness or disease, slap a generic "natural causes" tag to their files and call it a day. Life would carry on, just like before. And no one would be any wiser as to what was really happening at Spring Lakes. What was happening in the field.

Beyond it.

"Okay," Kim said. "Yes, it's happened before. But never this many guests at once. That's why Lee called you. He thought it was a disease maybe, something that could be transferable to the other patients. We panicked, and, well, here we are."

"You knew something was wrong before and you continued to let it go on. For how long, Kim?"

"I didn't know anything was wrong, not at first." Her somber appearance and quiet inflection were enough to convince Amanda she wasn't lying. Or, at least, that she believed her own bullshit.

Barnes stepped forward. "Don't cry innocence. What about your predecessor? Don't tell me he didn't know about the other sixty-niners, that he didn't tell you about what was happening here."

"He said nothing to me." She shook her head adamantly, her face long and drawn. Amanda thought she might cry. "I never met him. He killed himself a month before I took over this facility."

"I'm sorry?" Amanda unfolded her arms. "Killed himself?"

Kim shot Phelps a nasty look. "Didn't discover that in your little research mission?"

Phelps shook her head.

"Yes," Kim continued, looking increasingly uneasy. "Killed himself. Right in this office, actually. Overdosed on blood pressure medication. Took over fifty pills. An assistant found him the very next morning. No note. No nothing."

"Jesus fuck," Barnes said, leaning on the wall for support.

"You believe us?" asked Amanda. She squinted as if trying to get a better look into the woman's eyes, as if the truth evaded her there. "About the field? You believe us, don't you?"

Kim glanced about the room. "I..."

Amanda slammed her fist down on the table, causing a few stationary items to jump. "Do you believe us?"

"I... I've never seen anything remotely close to what you've described."

Amanda got the sense she was being lied to. "But others have claimed to? See things? Out there?"

Kim didn't reject this. Her eyes continued to bounce between the three of them.

"Who?" asked Phelps.

Kim closed her eyes, as if wishing to be done with this whole thing. The situation clearly weighed heavily on her shoulders, and she was quickly losing the strength to deal. "Some of the... of the *sixty-niners,* as you call them... had claimed to have experienced... *things...* leading up to their deaths."

"What kinds of things?" Amanda demanded to know.

"Visions. Seeing things that weren't there. Ghosts. Some claimed their dreams intensified. They came in the form of memories. Past things they'd done. Traumatic life events."

"Give me examples."

Kim frowned, then went for the folder. She plucked out the article near the top. "This woman," she said, pointing to the photograph of the deceased guest, her smiling face. "Amber. She... she had been attacked by a dog when she was little. Said she needed over a hundred stitches. Claimed a dog came to visit her over the weeks leading up to her... *uh-hem*—death. Not just any dog, mind you. The *same* dog. The German Shepard that had ripped apart her legs. She began to see it everywhere. In her room. In the halls. Outside, across the street. Also, she said every time it came near, she felt phantom pain near where she'd been stitched up."

"And this woman," Barnes said, "she ended up exactly like the others? Paralyzed, but still alive?"

Kim nodded. "For approximately twenty-four hours. Then, she... uh... *expired.*"

"The others," Amanda said, flipping through the contents of the folder, scanning each victim's name and face. "The same? Similar experiences? Visions? Dreams? Identical deaths?"

"Yes. All the same. Except for this time. They've always gone, as far as I can tell, one at a time. But now, it's all of them. Everyone aged sixty-nine."

Amanda turned to the others. "I wonder why."

Barnes shrugged. "Maybe it's been experimenting up until now. Seeing what it can get away with? Now, maybe it's expanding its reach a little."

Kim shook her head. "We don't even know what it is. If there even is an *it*. Who's to say it still isn't some disease? Something that attacks the brain like some advanced, never-been-discovered form of Alzheimer's?"

The three of them craned their heads toward the facility's director.

Though Amanda enjoyed the theory of a super, fast-acting form of Alzheimer's affecting a small portion of the facility's populous, she couldn't buy into it, mostly because of what she'd seen in the field. There was no scientific explanation for what was happening. Nothing medical. This whole thing was...

Unearthly.

Amanda replied first. "I can assure you that what we've witnessed isn't some undiscovered sickness or disease, or some variation of a degenerative brain condition."

"She still doesn't believe us," Barnes added. "And I get that sentiment. I really do. It's not an easy pill to swallow, but you have to look at all the evidence here. *All* of it. That includes what you can see with your own eyes." He motioned to the folder, documented proof that something *un*natural was taking place at Spring Lakes. "There is something wrong here, Kim, and the longer you deny it, the longer you don't admit that we have a major fucking issue, the more people are going to get hurt. Like *Cunningham* kind of hurt. You feel me?" When she didn't respond right away, he added, "People will die, Kim. People will fucking die."

She seemed to scan his thoughts. "What makes you believe so easily? What makes you think what you saw out there was real? I mean," she scoffed, "do you honestly expect me to believe you saw a man out there? A man who showed you things? A monster in the trees?"

"I trust my eyes, Kim. And my brain, and its ability to recognize the difference between reality and fantasy, and what happened out there in the field—that was fucking real."

"Ask Cunningham how real it was if you don't believe us," Amanda snapped.

Kim chewed on her tongue, and Amanda could only imagine the venomous words that were resting there. "Okay," she said, dropping her intimidating pose. "Suppose it *is* real. All of it. Every word." She looked at them, surveying their faces, as if trying to seek out leverage, something she could use to swing the conversation—the debate of reality versus fantasy—in her favor. "What does it want and how do we stop it?"

Amanda opened her mouth to speak, but then she realized she didn't have an answer. She was about to tell them they needed to work it out, piece together whatever information they had and come to an agreement, a well-informed decision, when Phelps spoke up.

"It seems to see into our memories," she said. "The thing in the field, it can look inside our heads... dig up the past, make us see things we don't particularly want to see. It uses our memories against us, almost as a weapon, and I think... I don't know... I *feel* like it may feed off them. I think it lives off that. And it has lived off that for a very long time. Maybe even before this facility was built."

"So..." Kim said, placing her fingers on her temples, trying to wrap her mind around Phelps's theory. "It's feeding on the memories of the people here?"

"And anyone who gets too close. In our case, I think it felt threatened by our presence. It lashed out and attacked, thus, what happened to Cunningham."

Amanda snapped her fingers and pointed at Phelps. "That's a great theory and all, and I'm not saying you're wrong, but that still doesn't explain the significance of sixty-nine, though. Why it chooses to touch those people when it can very clearly have its way with anyone else."

She nodded. "Sixty-nine-year-olds aren't the only ones that can be affected, hence, our own experiences. I think it *chose* those people because of their age. The number."

"Yeah, but why?"

"I have a theory about that too, actually."

"Oh, this oughta be good," Kim said, rolling her eyes, clearly not completely buying into the conjecture being so casually tossed around. Everyone ignored her.

"Sixty-nine is a significant, popular number, and probably for all the reasons you can imagine, something I'm not going to explore here—but use your brains, the infantile portions, and figure it out for yourself. But regardless of *that* aspect, the number sixty-nine is often viewed as the *yin-and-yang* of the number world, a number that represents duality, yet an interconnectedness. It could represent a relationship, a marriage between two individuals, two separate entities coming together and joining, becoming one in the spiritual sense. Opposites that unite, interact and take on a form all on its own, greater than what was envisioned individually. It could mean that, or it could mean a sense of balance, a *choice,* two options that lead us to the same destination. It could mean fate.

"I like the first idea better, though," she said, sounding confident in her assumption. "I think the notion that this thing needs us to become whole, borrow from us, consume our memories, fits with the number sixty-nine and what it says on the whole yin-and-yang aspect. Opposing forces coming together for the greater good."

"The greater good?" Kim scoffed, again, and her three visitors were starting to become numb to the sound. "Excuse me if I missed the section of your prattle where you mentioned the good in all of this. People are being tormented here for Christ's sakes. Dying. I've got an entire staff and guests who are terrified out of their wits, have no idea how to explain or rationalize what's happening to their loved ones, people they care about. Tell me, Miss Phelps, where is the greater good in that?"

"I think there's something else out there," Phelps said, turning and addressing Amanda and Barnes. "The something in the woods... the thing we couldn't quite see but know it's there... something that's big... something that's *dangerous.*"

Amanda felt a chill run up her arms as she recalled what she'd seen near the tree line, that amorphous white shape that brushed through the edge of the forest.

"You guys both saw it. I know you did. We didn't know what it was, not at the time, but, now, I think I know."

Amanda continued to see past the field, beyond the rows of tall grass. At the time she'd been so scared of the thing that posed as her grandfather that she hadn't had time to worry about what was out there, lingering near the tree line. Everything had happened so fast her brain couldn't catch up to the madness. But there was something there, she was sure of it, among the trees. Something waiting. Something hungry. Something that didn't feed on memories, or dreams of memories.

Something with teeth.

"What was it, Phelps?"

"I think it was the *enemy*."

"The enemy?" Amanda looked to Barnes and he only shrugged as if to say, *I have no idea what she's talking about either.*

"Yes. I think the true enemy is the thing in the forest, beyond the field. In a way, I think the field is protecting us from it. It's using us, a certain selected number of individuals, the sixty-niners, and taking their memories, draining them, stealing them, their lives, and it's turning their thoughts and mental images into energy, thus using that energy to protect us from whatever is out there beyond the field." She gasped for air, looking relieved to have gotten all that out. "You know, the yin-and-yang of it all. A balance. That's all it is, I think. Just balance. Just sixty-nine.

"And when we went out there to explore it, The Field, we disturbed it. Threatened it. Threatened that balance that could have been in place for centuries, maybe longer. Maybe forever. We threatened and it lashed out. Attacked us. Protected itself, and the balance."

No one spoke right away.

Phelps's enthusiasm faded when the silence lingered.

Kim squirmed in her chair. "I can't be a part of this... *lunacy.* How on Earth could you possibly know all of this? Or Christ, even think it up?"

"Never claimed to *know* anything," Phelps responded, plucking the cigarette out from behind her ear. "It's just a hunch. A guess. A theory. I've done some research using what we saw out there, explored what I *felt,* and this is what I've come up with. Just a hypothesis."

"It's crap."

Barnes put up his hand. "Now hold on just a sec. I like to think of myself as a realist. I don't go around believing any old thing. I don't believe in magic, ghosts, and no god has ever appealed to me, made me want to get on my knees and give praise. But what we witnessed out there... really shook me. Everything we've seen here has been... just *too much*. Too much for me to disregard what Phelps is trying to tell me, however impossible it may sound. Now, I don't know that I necessarily agree with everything she said, but... I don't know, there's a part of me that... *agrees*. It feels *right*."

"I still don't understand *sixty-nine*," Amanda said, following along. "You're saying this thing... it just likes the significance of the number and that's why it chooses to prey on the people here? How does a thing like that understand numbers, their supposed significance?"

Phelps bit her lip, let go of it, then popped the smoke into her mouth. "No. Yes. Maybe. What I'm saying is this thing, The Field, it *recognizes* the number's significance. How that's possible is beyond our understanding at this time. But I think it chooses its—let's call them sacrifices—*because* of the number. Sixty-nine to us is just that—a number. It holds no significance beyond that. That's just how old these people are. To us, it's as meaningless as if they were sixty-eight or seventy. But, to this thing, it's not just a number. It's something else. It's what these people are. They *are* sixty-nine. To the universe, in the scope of cosmic numerology, that defines these people—their age, their number. Sixty-nine gives this thing power, and this thing has chosen these people's existence, their length of life on this earthly plane, to draw from. Take that however you want, dissect it, sift through it, but the evidence... the evidence is there, man." She pointed at the folder, teeming with articles, to demonstrate her point.

Kim, still doubtful, shook her head. "This is utter nonsense. And I won't—no, *can't*—be a part of it. The three of you, from here on out, are on your own."

Amanda turned to her. "Newsflash, bitch. You *are* a part of it. In fact, I think you've helped perpetuate this thing."

Kim's face blanched at Amanda's language. "How dare you speak to me like that? Who do you think you are? All of you—what gives you the right to disrespect me and what—"

"All right, all right," Barnes said, stepping in and waving his hands like a referee. "We don't need to rip each other apart—that thing out there is doing a good enough job of that as it is. What we need to do is put our heads together and figure out a way to eradicate this thing and save these people before their time is up."

"Sounds great," Phelps said, sucking on her unlit cigarette. "But one question, though—if indeed my theory is correct, why would we want to stop something that is protecting us from something that's a far greater threat to our existence?" Phelps arched her brow. "Why would we want to contribute to our own destruction?"

"Because one, as tantalizing and well-spoken as your theory may be, we don't know it's one-hundred percent true. It's just speculation right now, and I mean that respectfully."

"Finally, some sense-talking," Kim interjected, but Barnes went on ignoring her.

"That's all it is right now, that's all *any* of this talk is. And two..." He shrugged as if he'd given up trying to explain things. "Because people are dying, Phelps. And we have to protect them. That's what we do. Even if your theory ends up being true, we can't sit idly by and watch, *allow*, people to die. We can't. If some infectious disease came along and threatened the planet, would we let it kill thousands just to save everyone? No, we wouldn't. We would find a way to save the thousands and everyone else; not only because that's our job, but because that's the right thing to do. We save people. Every single one we can."

Phelps bit down on the filter, seemingly unconvinced by Barnes's speech.

Kim waved her hands in the air. "Do whatever you want. But leave me and my staff out of it. Come tomorrow, these people will be dead and that'll be the end of it."

"Until next year, when it kills more of them," Amanda said. "And the year after that. And the year after. On and on, until the end of time. What then?"

Kim showed them her palms, raised her shoulders. "That's life. People die. In here, it happens all the time. So it goes."

"That's a great way of looking at life, Kim. You should be really proud of yourself."

A smirk pulled the woman's lips to one side. "Life is death, Mrs. Guerrero. Life is death."

17

RESTING WITH HER elbows on the handicap ramp's railing, Phelps puffed out an enormous cloud of cigarette smoke. The early afternoon sun hung high in the sky; the orange globe providing her with the warmth she needed to battle the chills. She wasn't getting sick but found herself unable to shake the icy bugs that continuously skittered across her flesh. Smoking her cigarette down to the filter, she turned and saw Barnes and Amanda stepping through the back door, both looking like they'd just lost a war.

"We gonna do this?" Phelps asked, the question itself spawning another round of shivers.

Amanda nodded. "That bitch won't be of any help. We're on our own from here on out. She wants no part of it, won't even ask the other security guard to accompany us."

"Can't say I blame her on that account," Barnes said, opening his palm, begging Phelps for his own smoke. She gave him his pick of the pack. Didn't take him long to pop the thing in his mouth and spark the tip. "In fact, it might be better if it was just the three of us. No sense dragging another innocent life into this mess."

"Still," Amanda said, pacing the concrete walk. "It'd be nice if we had another witness. Someone with *some* authority."

"I don't think it likes authority," Phelps blurted out. She lighted her second cigarette in a row and it tasted almost as good as the first, a rare instance. "The Field, I mean. It targeted the guard, right? I mean, none of us were harmed. Then, we went into the woods with Kim and the cops, and we couldn't even find the thing. It was like it wanted to keep a low profile. It wants to operate in secret, even though the nature of its existence doesn't allow that to happen, fully, since it needs to feed on the sixty-niners. It needs people to survive but likes to feed quietly. Maybe that's why it's only been taking one a year, or every other."

(our secret)

(one a year)

(to avoid suspicion)

"Then why seven now?"

Barnes suggested, "Maybe it's hungrier. A growing boy needs his lunch."

Phelps blew smoke out through her nostrils. "Maybe the thing it's protecting us from is getting stronger. Maybe it needs more power to fight it off. To prevent it from escaping."

Amanda turned her head at this.

"Whatever its purpose, whatever its reasons, one thing is for sure—so far, we've gone after it twice and it hasn't tried to harm *us*. Cunningham was an outlier. It didn't even attack the two cops that came with us the second time."

"Then why Cunningham, I wonder," Barnes said, smoke fogging before him.

Phelps thought back to the moment when Cunningham was about to use his baton. "Maybe it felt threatened by Cunningham. He had a weapon."

"The baton," Amanda said, almost a whisper.

"Exactly. I got the sense he was itching to use that thing."

"So, it felt threatened and lashed out." Amanda looked at the two of them, studied their expressions. "You don't think us going out there for a third time, with the intentions of stopping it, is going to put it in defense mode."

Phelps arched her left eyebrow. "I don't really know."

Barnes pinched the cig between his teeth and grimaced. "I still don't understand why it didn't just try to kill us the first time. Surely it had to know we weren't bringing it early Christmas presents."

Phelps shook her head, staring off into space. "Maybe it needs something from us. Maybe it wanted us to see." It made sense to her, that the thing in the field exclusively made itself visible to them, or, as visible as it could. She kept picturing the anatomically inaccurate version of her grandmother lying on the hospital bed, her arms dangling at impossible lengths, wearing a smile of pure evil design. She pictured the thing lifting her grandmother's arms, reaching for her. Fingers that were gnarled like old roots.

(our secret)

(killed them all)

(all the boys)

The hair on her arms went fully erect. What she'd seen out there felt so damn real, even though she knew it was all an elaborate mirage, something The Field projected before them. Something only meant for their innocent eyes. They'd all seen different things, experienced alternate past truths. It stood to reason that The Field had access to their minds, was able to leaf through their memories like a child's picture book. "Maybe it wants us to help it?"

"Help it do what?"

Phelps had burned through half her cigarette, decided it had lost all its allure and threw the butt into the collector next to the garbage can. "Maybe the sixty-niners aren't enough. Maybe the thing in the woods is getting stronger, and the sixty-niners simply aren't working anymore. It needs more. More of... more memories." She turned to them now, her eyes sparkling with new ideas behind them. "That's why it took *all* of the sixty-niners this time, instead of just one. Maybe it's getting more powerful and The Field needs more energy, more power, to fight it.

"And it needs us, needs our tragic moments to help."

Barnes and Amanda exchanged looks.

"I don't know, Phelps," Amanda finally said, after a few seconds of breathless silence. "I think we're jumping to all sorts of crazy conclusions."

Phelps's gaze targeted the ground. "Yeah, you're probably right. I just... I have all these feelings inside me."

"Feelings?" asked Barnes, who was savoring every last hit of nicotine. He smoked the thing like he wanted it to never end—slow, inhaling deeper with each pull.

"Yeah, what I saw out there in the field... it really shook me. I mean, that thing dug deep."

"We all saw things out there, Phelps. It got to all of us."

"That's not what I mean. It's like... whatever it did to me when it had its look inside... I feel like it *left* something there. Like a seed. And every second spent here, at Spring Lakes, its watering that seed, letting it grow." She looked up at them, wondering if they felt the same way. "Do you guys... feel that?"

If they did, no one admitted it.

"I think we need to be smart about this," Amanda said, addressing Barnes more-so than Phelps. Phelps wondered if she had talked too much, revealing too many of her feelings. She'd never been good at that, never been inclined to share personal tidbits, but she felt a closeness to Barnes and Amanda, a trust. *Connected.* She truly felt she could confide in them, and maybe that was because of what had happened out there, what they'd seen—but then again, maybe it wasn't. Maybe she just *felt* like their friends, and she was putting too much stock in their professional relationship. "I say we go out there with no intent to *do* anything. Just watch. Observe. Take notes. See if it... if it *contacts* us again. And take it from there."

"And what if it decides to kill us?" Barnes asked, a question Phelps hadn't given much thought. The thing, as horrifying as the images it had projected were, as terrifying as the form it had taken, hadn't felt dangerous. Not to her. Though, the facts remained—it had taken lives. Almost a dozen of them, the sixty-niners of Spring Lakes, over the last thirty years. There was no news on Cunningham, but given the extent of the man's injuries, it was unlikely he'd make a full recovery. At the very least, he was bound to become half the human being he was when he began work that day. Who knew if his mind would ever recover from the atrocities he'd been shown, the stuff that caused him to put out his own eye?

"I don't think it will do that," replied Amanda. "Not if we don't show aggression. Phelps, would you agree?"

Phelps nodded.

Barnes looked them twice over, pausing as if he needed more convincing. "You have more confidence in that thing than I do. I don't think we should walk out there without being prepared."

"Prepared for what?"

"To fight."

Amanda shook her head. "No."

"It doesn't want to kill us," Phelps told him.

But Barnes wasn't having any of it. "You don't know that. You don't. I'm sorry—all of this sounds good, great in fact, but when you break it all down, the simple fact is that you don't know any more or less about that thing out there than I do. Or Kim Charon does. Or Cunningham. Or the residents of Spring Lakes. The Field is dangerous, and we shouldn't buy into the fact that it spared us once. Who's to say that will happen again?"

Phelps and Amanda didn't have an answer for that.

"Right," Barnes added, after the women had failed to produce concrete evidence to support their theory. "Then we'll need weapons."

"Weapons will only antagonize it," Phelps said with broken confidence. "The fact we didn't have weapons the first time was the difference between us and Cunningham."

Barnes tilted his head back, facing the sky. She could see he was frustrated over his voice not being heard. But she'd heard him loud and clear.

She just strongly disagreed.

"No weapons," Phelps said. "We go without weapons or we don't go at all."

"You sound so sure of yourself that it's starting to freak me out." Barnes discarded his cigarette in the sand-filled pail next to the door.

More confident now than she had ever been before, she nodded. "I am."

"So, what's the plan then?" Amanda asked. Her voice was far from calm. Phelps noticed her hands were shaking, though she tried hiding them by shoving them into her pockets. "I mean, what do we do? I hate to say it, but, if this thing *is* protecting us, why do anything at all?"

Barnes clicked his tongue. "You know why, Amanda. We just had this conversation inside. You wanna jump on Kim Charon's side of the fence?"

Amanda shot him a look, one that read *maybe I do*. Phelps couldn't blame her for thinking such things, especially given the nature of their future and the decisions they'd need to make. She had voiced the possibility of turning her head from the situation too, as much as she didn't want to.

"Obviously we can't let it continue to take the lives of the people here," Phelps said, changing her tune. "Maybe there is something else we can offer it in their place."

Barnes threw his hands up. "This is sounding more bat-shit nuts by the second."

"You have a better idea, Barnes?"

"Yeah, I do." He held up the book of matches he'd taken from the bar earlier. "Let's burn this motherfucking forest to the ground. Kill two birds with one stone. Take out The Field and whatever the fuck is beyond it."

Phelps's brow arched high up on her forehead. "You boys. Always want to set the world on fire. You really think striking a match will hurt this thing?"

"It's worth a shot."

Amanda came forward. "No, it's not. With our luck, the winds would blow the flames back toward Spring Lakes, or into the nearby town. I'm not doing that. I have enough weighing on my conscience right now. I don't need the deaths of a few hundred people on top of them."

"Then what?"

Phelps cleared her throat, shot them a look that would have given goosebumps to anyone with a pulse. "We talk to it. Reason with it. We give it whatever it wants."

No one offered a better solution that didn't involve putting their or anyone else's lives at risk. Phelps's went over the rest of her plan as they headed back inside to prepare for their trek out into The Field.

18

AS SOON AS they stepped foot on the path, an intimidating sense of dread draped over Amanda's shoulders, squeezing her from the inside out. She felt this magnetic pull coming from deep within the woods, a mystical something that was drawing her back to the field. She wanted to open her mouth, ask the others if they had developed the same trepidation, but unlocking her jaw proved difficult.

The forest looked different this time around. The trees were more bent, less sturdy than they'd appeared only hours earlier; as if they'd been uprooted during a big storm and were a breeze away from crashing to the leave-covered soil. As they traveled deeper, the foliage became denser, lusher. The trees had been pretty bare during their first and second walk, but now they were full of life, an explosion of green and yellow tones. It was as if seasons had passed between visits. Sunlight filtered in through the leaves, sequestering shadows and providing the path with a generous amount of visibility. Bushes were nice and round, the branches cloaked with leaves and flowering buds. Birdsong echoed from a distance, all around them, the tweets bringing with them a sense of comfort and familiarity, harbingers of fortunate outcomes. The path was less obtrusive than it had previously been, with almost no overgrowth blocking their way. The terrain was even, as if the path had been manmade, smoothed for ease of access. They got about half a mile before Amanda began to question whether they were on the same path as before, if they had unknowingly entered the woods through another entry point or had made a wrong turn somewhere.

But she reassured herself that that wasn't the case, mostly because there was only one entry point and no turns to speak of.

And no one else seemed to notice these things. If they did, no one spoke up. In fact, no one had said much at all, about anything. It was as if talking had been forbidden on their journey.

As they walked, venturing farther into their bright-green surroundings, Amanda noticed a little fig bush just off the path, maybe twenty paces. The sight stole her attention immediately, and she stopped in her tracks, stared off into the short distance as if a ghost had stood in that very place. The others didn't take notice of her abrupt stop and continued on, without her. The fig bush was in full bloom, and the figs were ripe, had reached the final stages of their growth. She migrated over to the bush, and, as soon as she left the path, another feeling cozied up with her. This one seemed harmless as the rest, though it did make her a little uneasy. Eyes, she felt. A thousand of them on her, carefully probing her movements, documenting every second. She glanced around the wooded area, examining the spaces between every tree and bush, and saw nothing, not a single eye in view. She even looked up at the sky, browsed the tops of the trees, combed every visible branch to see if there were *watchers* up there, but alas, her own eyes came away with nothing. There was no one there, no one at all, only the sense of a thousand sentinels keeping track of her every step. Every twitch. Every breath.

Her blood froze then, but she was in front of the fig tree now, close enough to reach out and pluck free one of the fat fruit sacks, if she wished. And she did wish that, wished it very much. She reached out for one in particular, a juicy red-brown nugget that was almost bursting at the seam with that delicious sweet-berry flavor.

Her family had kept a fig tree in the backyard when she was little. Every year, her father would reap anywhere from twenty to thirty figs. Her mother would make snacks with them, breakfast bars and cookies. She'd eat them with cereal. They'd have them as dessert after a big dinner. Her family had bonded over those figs. As she got older, the fig tree stopped producing. Maybe her father hadn't taken care of it in those later years. Maybe they had begun to care less and less about it. Which was strange because, when she thought about it, that was exactly what had happened to her. They'd stopped paying attention to her. Stopped giving her money, weekly allowances so she could go hang out with friends. Stopped buying her food and groceries. Stopped funding her college account. They hadn't even offered to co-sign her student loans, and flat-out refused to when she approached them about it.

She'd become the fig tree.

And she knew why.

(touch it)

She had told them about her *abuelo,* the filthy things he'd made her do. The things that, when she'd finally mustered the guts to come forth and tell her truth, made her gag. Acid burned the back of her throat when she thought of those things, the images from all those moments, those memories of weekends spent at her grandfather's, those vile acts he had forced upon her—*thinking* caused that, so speaking about what had happened had made her physically ill. After she had spoken her truth, she had emptied her stomach on her parents' kitchen floor. Her stomach. Her heart. Her brain. After she had finished, she had felt nothing but hollow inside. A shell of the human being she truly was.

Of course, her parents hadn't believed her. They had gone so far as to call her a liar, a terrible person, someone who should feel ashamed for spouting these horrendous accusations, because, after all, that was all they were—*accusations*—and how dare she do that to someone who loved her, had done nothing but be there for her and take care of her. *Play with her.*

(touch it)

They had told her not to speak another word about this to them or anyone, ever again, and, if she did, that they would disown her, cut her from their lives as if she were nothing, some common acquaintance—*her*, their only daughter.

And she didn't speak of it again. To a therapist some odd years later, but not anyone else, ever again. And it was funny—well, not funny, *sad* actually, fucking heartbreaking—but even though she had never spoken a word of what her grandfather had done to her behind his office doors, things he had made her touch and stimulate, stroke and swallow, her parents had abandoned her anyway. After she had confided in them, after she had finally harnessed enough courage to come forth, after years and years of keeping it inside, locked away, after she had finally built the strength to tell her folks the goddamn truth, they had immediately written her off. Not just her truth, but her life. Her truth meant nothing to them, and her life—well, that apparently meant very little. She'd become a stain to them, something that couldn't be washed off with soap and water or cleansed with bleach. Something they'd carry around with them forever, a burden that kept on giving.

They couldn't have that; it was easier to cut the cord.

She hated them for it. For everything. They had meant nothing to her since then, and they meant even less now. Just a memory, like a bad dream you experienced when you were a child; there, somewhere in the distance, but mostly forgotten.

But the figs were the last good image she had of them. And so, she had held onto that throughout the years, the mental snapshot of the fig bush in the backyard, the one that bloomed so beautifully come springtime.

She let a cluster of three figs dangle on her palm. Running her fingers over their velvety skin, she tried to remember what they'd tasted like. Sweet, yes. Almost berry-like, but squishy like a banana. And full of seeds. She remembered spending ten to fifteen minutes in front of the mirror, picking seeds out from between her teeth, her father behind her dangling a long strand of floss, his belly shaking with laughter as she tried to pinch the seeds with her tiny fingers.

She chose one of the figs, the biggest of the trio, and plucked it from the branch. Placing it beneath her nose, she sniffed, taking in the sticky-sweet aroma. She closed her eyes and saw her father hunched over, pointing out which figs were ready for mother's cookies, and the seven-year-old version of herself dancing around the fig tree, plucking each ripe one he'd given her permission to take.

When she opened her eyes, it was just her and the fig and the still forest. The birdsong had faded some, was still there, but not as present. Instead, there was this low hum, this drone that continued to buzz in the background, slowly becoming prominent over the rest of the forest's tunes. Soon, that was all she heard; everything else had gone silent except the drone.

The fig called to her.

Begged to be eaten.

Almost as if she didn't want to, she brought the fig to her lips. Opened her mouth. Put the fig between her teeth. Bit do—

Something smacked her hand, hard enough to send a shot of pain up her arm. The fig went sailing into the nearby brush and got lost amongst the fallen, dead leaves.

"What are you doing?" Barnes asked, now standing next to her. He'd come, seemingly from nowhere, as if he'd materialized from the ether of some surreal nightmare.

She rubbed her hand, the pain traveling, causing her fingers to tingle. "You... hit me."

"You were going to eat something. From the forest."

Behind Barnes, Phelps stood on the path. She hadn't stepped foot off the even surface, and she didn't look as if she intended to.

"So?" Amanda asked. The figs attracted her eyes. An overwhelming urge to stuff a handful of them in her mouth entered her mind, and she found the desire hard to shake. "So what?"

She reached out again, and this time Barnes grabbed her hand. "Amanda, no."

Amanda fought him with little energy. Her weak attempt to grab at the fig tree was easily defeated by Barnes's strength. The irresistible urge that she needed a fig, needed one in her mouth, needed to bite down and flood her tongue with its juicy flavor, suddenly conquered her mind and, for a second, that was all she cared about. It was as if nothing else existed but that phantom taste. The desire was so strong she seriously considered kicking Barnes between the legs, giving his testicles a little more than a love tap. That feeling only intensified the longer she kept the tree in her sights. And then, in that exact moment, she knew the figs and the tree were bad. Not only bad, but poison.

Poison for the mind, she thought.

She broke free from Barnes's grip, and, instead of reaching out, plucking a delicious afternoon snack from one of Earth's most precious treasures, she ran, scrambled her way back up the small incline, back toward the path where Phelps was waiting for her with open arms. She grabbed her hand and with Barnes's help from behind, made her way back to even terrain.

Once back on the path, she could hear the fig tree calling to her. Not with words or a song, nothing she could hear, but something she could *feel.* In her mind. As if whatever had put the damned thing there had done so just for her, and touching it, putting her fingers on a single fig, had granted the thing access to her. To her thoughts.

The image of the tree kept flashing in her head, over and over again, toggling back and forth between the one she'd just seen and the one that existed in her parents' yard. And, as she separated the two, or as the thing did so for her, she began to realize that they were, in fact, the same fucking tree. The same. *Exact.* One.

"*Impossible,*" she said, the words falling out in a breath.

"What's that?" Barnes asked. "What did you see out there?"

She looked away from the tree, which still appeared closer than she felt it ought to. "You..."

"All I saw was you reaching out and grabbing something. It looked like you were going to put something in your mouth, so I just... reacted."

Amanda turned back to where the tree was, but now wasn't. In its place was a small mound of dead leaves, the top of the pile moving due to a gentle breeze that had streaked through the forest. No tree. No figs. No evidence that there ever was one.

"It was just there," Amanda said, and she hated how manic her voice sounded. How panicked she had become. She hadn't heard her own voice strain that way since... well, a very long time.

(touch it)
(mom, dad, why don't you believe me)
(touch it)
(he did things to me)
(touch it)
(he abused me)

She felt her face grow wet with tears. Phelps pulled her close, hugged her. She cried into her shoulder, soaking the fabric of her sweatshirt.

Barnes kept his hand on her back, his touch filling her with a sense of comfort. A sense of warmth. Something good. The vibe conquered her body, killing the panic, the stress, everything the fig tree had gifted her.

They remained huddled for what seemed like a very long time.

19

I T TOOK A few tries, but Barnes was finally able to convince the girls to keep moving. He didn't want to linger too long in one spot. One reason was that time was precious—though, he did have a sneaking suspicion that time worked differently in the woods and the closer they got to the field. He had gathered that much from their last excursion. The second (and more important) reason was that he didn't like how it felt when they weren't moving. Standing still, he could... *feel* things.

It was hard to explain, and, even to himself, it sounded ludicrous. But it was kind of like being tickled, only the source of the tickling—the tickl*er*, if you will—was coming from inside him. Inside his head. His brain. He felt it moving when they weren't, but, as they walked, he felt nothing. He liked feeling nothing. Nothing felt normal. Safe.

After hiking about a mile and not coming upon the field, the place they'd been so sure was "just a little farther", Barnes stopped and turned to them. "Something isn't right. We should have been there by now."

The girls swapped concerned glances.

Amanda, whose face had dried, surveyed the trees, seemingly mindful of what her eyes might show her. "I don't get it. Why is it keeping us away?"

Phelps shook her head. "It's not. I think it's feeding off us right now."

Barnes hated the way that sounded, though it would explain the tickling sensation that was patrolling his head. A cold trail ran down his spine. "I can feel something."

"In your head? Moving about?"

He nodded.

"That's how it starts, I think. First the feeling. Then... I don't know... you start... seeing things."

"Seeing things?" His arms hardened with tiny bumps.

"Images. Things in your mind. Then..."

"They become real," Amanda finished for her. "That's the way it was with the fig tree."

Barnes shook his head. "No, that... that isn't possible."

Amanda rolled her eyes. "Oh, shut up, Barnes. You know damn well it is. You saw what the field showed us, and you saw what the note showed you. Don't start playing the role of disbeliever, not now. It's too late for that shit."

Barnes hung his head. "I know... I wasn't. I'm just trying to convince myself that this isn't really happening, that none of this is. And maybe, if we believe it, maybe we can make it so. Maybe it will all go away."

The girls only stared at him.

"Okay, fine. It was stupid. Stupid thinking." He was sweating and it wasn't particularly hot outside.

Amanda faced Phelps. "What did you see, Phelps?"

Her eyes scanned the trees, and she squinted as if the thing she'd seen was still there, only hiding now. "I saw..."

A beat of pure silence, and then came the subtle sound of leaves brushing against each other in the soft, late-afternoon breeze.

"Go on, Phelps. Tell us."

"I saw... her."

"Who's her?" asked Barnes, ignoring the intrusive images that kept flashing before him. His dead lover lying in the grass outside of the public restroom, his face beaten bloody and unrecognizable, looking like a body mold from a low-budget horror movie. He blinked and Brian was gone, and three seconds later, Brian was back again, dead like always. "Phelps?"

"Her... my grandmother... the boys..."

Phelps turned and stared past them, down the path. As if there was something there. Barnes saw nothing but the bend in the path, the one that would lead them down another stretch of trees and memories, but no field. The Field, Barnes thought, was becoming something they'd seen once and weren't allowed to see again.

"The boys she killed, I can see their faces," Phelps said distantly and dream-like. It reminded Barnes of how Brian used to mumble-speak in his sleep, say things that made no sense, things he couldn't remember saying come morning. "They're right there," she said, pointing to the path where Barnes, again, saw nothing but dirt and leaves and the promise of an exit from this awful place, this path that should not exist in nature. "They're right there and they're watching me. Smiling. Waving to me. They're waving me on, begging me to follow. They have things to show me, they say. They want to show me what she did to them. Those terrible things." She smiled and the briefest of laughs escaped her lips. "I know what they want. I know what they're after." She faced Barnes. "My sanity, what's left of it. But I won't go with them. We can't."

Barnes didn't see any boys, but he spotted a dark object hanging from one of the trees in the near distance, right about where the path took its bend. He began to walk toward it, but Phelps's voice stopped him.

"You can't do anything to them, Barnes. They won't listen to you."

He continued despite her claim. He had almost told her he wasn't going after them but decided not to waste his breath or the seconds, not that time mattered here anyway. After three steps, he heard Phelps tell Amanda that one of the boys had had all his limbs removed, how her grandparents had stripped his meat down to the bone. How the authorities had never found his body, yet, she knew that to be true. Oh, the horrific stories their rotting corpses would have told; if they had found them; if she had told someone.

Barnes walked toward the hanging object. As he got closer, he realized it wasn't a shadow and that it wasn't an object, not any old thing.

It was a person.

A human being.

Not just any person, though.

It was Brian.

And he was alive. Hanging there. Alive and looking well.

Well, not *well*. He looked like he had in the photos the cops showed him, when he'd been brought in to ID the body. His face was swollen and puffy like he'd been stung by a thousand hornets from hell. Barnes realized, above anything else, that he wasn't hanging from the tree—he was suspended in midair, floating between the branches and the ground, his arms and legs stretched as if he were a human five-pointed star. Barnes couldn't tell if Brian was smiling behind his bruised, inflated mask of a face, but he got the sense his lover was smiling, smiling as wide as the inflamed muscles and blood-swollen skin would allow.

Hey there, stud, the thing said, not with its mouth—but directly into his ear. As if Brian were right behind him instead of standing on an invisible ledge. Brian was unusually still for such a position, and that freaked out Barnes even more than the sudden appearance of his dead partner. Above anything else he'd witnessed, it was the stillness that really shook him.

Miss me?

"You know I do. So fucking much. Every fucking day."

Want to kiss me?

Barnes didn't answer that one. He knew the Brian staring down at him wasn't the one he'd kissed goodnight for four years, the one he'd cuddled to sleep every night.

"I know what you are," he told the thing. *The Field.* "I know exactly what you are."

I'm Brian. I'm... your love.

"No. You're not. You're just a cheap imitation. Just a memory. And not even my memory can do Brian justice."

For a brief second, Brian wasn't the way he'd been after the murderers were done with him. He was normal. He was wearing khakis and a nice silk button-down. It was the same outfit he'd worn to their first date. There wasn't a stain on it, not a speck of blood. His face was lean, his skin smooth—not grotesquely ballooned as it'd been moments ago. He was just... Brian. The way Barnes wished to remember him.

Tears tore down his face.

I'm Brian, the thing said again.

And Barnes wanted to believe him, he really did.

"You're... nothing."

I'm Brian. I'm Brian. I'm Brian.

"You're—"

I'M BRIAN. I'M BRIAN. I'M BRIAN.

Barnes dropped to his knees and covered his ears. The thing kept shouting, over and over, and his hands weren't enough to block out the noise. It was *in* his head. He could have stuffed his ears with cotton and still the sound would have come through. It was *in* him, a *part* of him, and there was *nothing* he could do except deal with the thing shouting his partner's name over and over again, listen while the bullhorn went off inside his head, giving hell to his eardrums, making them vibrate, threatening him with permanent damage.

He felt hands on him. Arms hooked under his shoulders, lifting him from the earth. Upon their touch, the screaming came to an abrupt halt. He looked around, frantically, and realized the rescue had come from Phelps and Amanda. They were gripping him tightly, holding onto him, as if he were saving them as well just by being there.

Barnes pulled them closer, then faced the path Brian had been hovering above. Brian was gone now, not a shred of evidence that he'd been there remaining. But there was a new vision to behold, one that had been projected for his eyes only.

Brian was on the ground in the center of the path, no more than twenty-five feet from where the trio stood on six weary legs. His face was battered, blown-up, fresh from the assault. His body was limp, lifeless. A man with a switchblade in his hand dropped to one knee beside him. The carver's friend, fellow murderer, stood next to him holding a bloody baseball bat, gripping the rubber end with both hands. A surprising amount of blood dribbled off the fat end of the bat, the sweet spot that had been cracked across Brian's face a half dozen times.

Yeah, the man said, *do that faggot up.*

The man with the knife began to carve.

"It's not real," Barnes told himself, but his senses were failing him. In addition to watching the heinous acts of the worst people this world had to offer, two monsters Barnes would gladly watch take the needle after a just sentence, he also smelled the wet grass of that particular night, the distant smell of exhaust that had been delivered by midnight winds. He could hear cars in the distance, the occasional horn blaring. The silence that never followed. He saw, heard, and smelled it all, and he firmly believed that, if he were to reach out, he'd be able to touch the swollen mask that had become Brian's face. "It's not real," he convinced himself. "None of it is real."

"None of it is real," Phelps mimicked, and he wondered if she was seeing her grandmother, and if Amanda was seeing her ghosts too. He suspected they were circling similar nightmares, trapped in whatever memorable horrors The Field wanted to show them. Their pasts; however it wanted to twist them, however it wanted to weaponize their recollections.

"None of it is real," Amanda said. "None of it is real."

"None of it is real," Barnes said, closing his eyes to the surreal visions before him. The darkness welcomed him, and he was thankful for its presence.

When he opened his eyes a moment later, the visions were gone. The path was as it had been—empty and inviting.

In the distance, he saw an ominous gold glow radiating from somewhere just around the bend.

"The Field," Phelps said, and began running toward it.

Amanda followed.

And so did he.

20

A ROUND THE BEND, the path gave way to The Field. It lay as it had before. The lengthy straw grass stood to their shoulders. Beyond it existed a wide circular flat spot, a place where Amanda imagined some extraterrestrial spaceship touching down. Near the back edge of the flattened earth, a naked tree of medium height stood, its lifeless branches swaying in the soft breeze that kicked across the field. And beyond the lone tree stood a wall of them, the very ones she'd seen bend when a great and terrible figure had pushed its way through the woods—the thing Phelps suggested was the real enemy here and not the field itself, though, after what she'd witnessed on the path, she couldn't fully buy into Phelps's hunch.

Amanda pushed her way through the straw grass, releasing cottony dandelion spores airborne. She watched them glide through the air, floating like snow flurries on a dreary winter morning. Keeping her focus on the center of the field, the bald spot, she ignored everything else happening around her. She ignored the fact that the closer she got to the center, the funnier her head felt. As if someone had opened the top of her skull and was poking the jelly-like surface of her brain, prodding her dome like some archaic science experiment. She ignored that phantom sensation, and the...

...the presence.

There was something out there in the field with them, and the woods beyond. While she hadn't committed to Phelps's theory in full, there was certainly something out there, clad in shadows. Stalking. Lurking. Biding its time, waiting for the precise moment to spring forth and pounce on its prey.

And Amanda felt like prey. She was walking right into a trap. Yet, despite those feelings and premonitions of her demise, she continued on anyway, approaching the center of the clearing.

The dead tree swayed in a violent gust.

She dropped to her knees, waiting for The Field to show itself. Its true form.

Behind her, Phelps and Barnes followed, planting their knees in the mud-soft earth.

She blinked, and nighttime suddenly conquered the skies.

Her grandfather appeared before her, standing, his arms open as if he were trying to hug all three of them at once. *"You've come back to me..."*

"Yes," she said. "To end this."

Her grandfather hissed with laughter, a hideous sound that reminded her of a slashed tire.

"You cannot end what is endless, child."

"I know what you are," she told The Field. "You're a vampire. You feed on these people. On their memories. Eating them one at a time. The sixty-niners; they're your food. They nourish you."

The thing seemed pleased by her assumptions. *"You know nothing about me, child. The number of years I've existed are incalculable. I am all that exists here. I am The Field. I am Sixty-Nine."*

"That means nothing to me." She shook her head, staring into her grandfather's eyes. They were glowing, yellow, the eyes of a cat shrouded in darkness. "I came here... *we* came here... to reason with you. To beg you. To leave this place."

The thing dropped its smile, and she knew the answer without needing to hear its reply.

"I will never leave this place," it said, walking toward her. Its arms and legs moved without grace, like a child learning to find his feet. *"I am this place. It is me and I am it."*

Beyond the thing that could only be an illusion, that terrible featureless something moved in the woods, stirring amongst the trees. The treetops shimmied, shaking loose leaves over the ground below. The trunks arched, bending like fishing poles with sharks on the line. A gust of wind stormed across the field, nearly flattening the tall straw grass. The sky was dark and full of stars, bright spots living in an opaque world.

"Please," Amanda begged. "These people are innocent."

The thing laughed again, threw back its head. Its neck was abnormally long, and it had cocked its head so far back that Amanda thought its vertebrae would snap, its throat would split from the pressure. Somehow, probably the strange rules of this alternate world, the neck supported the weight of its bulbous head. Her grandfather's doppelganger righted itself, and then launched itself forward, hovering its face just over Amanda's head.

Amanda recoiled, her grandfather's image—The Field's version of it—leering at her from this proximity was all too much. Its lip curled as it growled like a guard dog, and that little act of aggression made her wonder if The Field *was* a guard dog. And whatever it was guarding was only just beyond it, that thing that prowled near the edge of the woods under a twilight universe.

Definitely two entities, she thought, wishing she could communicate with the others. She looked over her shoulder, saw Barnes and Phelps kneeling as they'd been before the sky had gone dark, only they were staring up at The Field with no eyes. They'd been snatched out of their sockets, replaced by two bleeding cavities, streaks of blood squirting down their faces. They didn't seem affected in the least, and they knelt in silence. Waiting. Watching. What the darkness had shown them, Amanda could only guess.

She was alone here. With *it*, The Field. And she felt it feeding off this notion, this moment, this experience. She was in its lair, in its palace of comfort, inside its dark territory, isolated from the others. Trapped. Forever bound to the thing's rotten whims. At its mercy, if it knew of such a word.

"I like the way your memories taste," it barked in her ear. She smelled something sweet, like dark licorice, only moldy. *"So delicious and sweet. Like a... like a fig from the finest tree."*

As it spoke, she tasted figs on her tongue; the sweet flavor, the crunch of the seeds between her teeth. She could smell her mother's baked treats, the pleasant aroma tantalizing her senses, freezing her skin. The gross licorice scent was gone, immediately forgotten. Then, a second later, it was all gone. Not just gone—but *gone*. From her memories. Extricated. The fresh-baked aromas, the images of her picking figs off the tree with her father beside her, pointing at every ripe fruit the branches offered. There was no more fig tree at all.

It had never existed.

A dark, blank block of space lived where the memories of those days had resided only moments ago.

She couldn't recall the figs or the tree she'd plucked them from, and, after a few moments, she'd forgotten what she couldn't remember altogether. As if there was really nothing there to begin with. A void where those memories should have been. A cavity of no-end, where eternal moments should be alive.

Surely there was something, she thought, but then began to doubt herself, doubted her own ability to access the past. Doubted her own brain and its ability to function properly. Was she losing it? Her mind?

Yes, she thought so. Though, it could have been the creature's doing.

She faced the smiling thing.

"Delicious indeed."

"What... what did you do to me?"

"Took a taste. Just a sample. And, oh my, how tasty. Your past is quite delectable. So good, I could eat your entire life in one bite."

She felt violated, and she didn't know exactly why. Her mind raced with all sorts of complex equations and conclusions, varying hypotheses on how this could happen to her, how she was able to see and feel what she was seeing and feeling. But in the end, she couldn't wrap her senses around it. The thing was inside her, sure, poking around, but what was it doing? What exactly had it come to do?

It came to eat, she told herself. *It came to feast.*

The thing glowed, a bright golden color. Her grandfather's image began to warp and twist, as did the world around it. She didn't know what was happening to her, but at the same time—she knew all too well.

No, she thought. *This can't be happening to me.*

The world was bleeding away from her. Her vision ran like thin paint. She reached behind her, to where she'd tucked the scissors she'd stolen from Kim Charon's desk, even though she was adamant about not bringing weapons, told the others to—under no circumstances— even *think* about bringing a weapon along, that weapons would only aggravate The Field. She was glad she had disobeyed her own command and brought along the scissors anyway, though she didn't know how useful they'd be in her fading state. She wasn't even sure she *could* use them, given how much the world was pulling itself apart before her very eyes.

Freeing the scissors from her belt, she immediately stabbed upward, near the direction she'd last seen her grandfather's glimmering eyes.

She felt the shears get stuck in something, and then a shrieking outburst stabbed her eardrums, temporarily deafening her. Something wet splattered on her hand, splashed against her cheeks, and even though the world looked like a kaleidoscope of melting rainbows, she knew what she'd felt was the thing's blood.

The Field's blood.

It bleeds, she thought. *The goddamn thing bleeds.*

She blinked and daylight flooded her eyes, driving her back, forcing her to bury her face in the crook of her arm.

She heard Barnes shouting. "No! No, don't do it! Please! God, no."

She uncovered her eyes and couldn't believe what she was seeing. It was Phelps. She was elevated, hanging in the sky, her limbs stretched tight in each direction, making her look like a human five-pointed star. She was crying blood; a red stream leaked from each eye, falling off her chin and puddling on the earthy surface below.

Amanda saw Phelps's mouth move, a weak attempt to communicate with them.

"Barnes! She's trying to talk!" Amanda shouted, and he stopped waving his arms and jumping up, trying to grab for her feet and pull her back down. It seemed the more he reached and protested her ascension, the higher she drifted away from them.

Looking up at her, he backed away.

"I..." Phelps said, the bloody tears falling more steadily now, red rivers of her eternal despair. "I... was... I was wrong."

And with that, she was quartered, each of her limbs ripped from their sockets by some malicious, invisible force, horses that simply weren't there. Blood spouted from where her arms and legs used to be, crimson geysers that arced into the air, rained down and watered the dead straw grass. She hung in limbo, all five pieces of her neither rising nor falling, and then, seconds later, she fell, all five pieces at once, to the blood-soaked earth.

Amanda screamed until her voice gave out.

Barnes folded forward and threw up.

Neither had time to grieve their loss; in the distance, near the edge of the forest, something large and ivory-white, a grotesque, hairless biped with spindly arms and legs, parted the trees and entered the field, its new domain, mouth hanging open—*impossibly* wide—and hungry for the meal it was currently being presented. White tusks, the length of the average human forearm, protruded from beneath its fat, whiskered upper lip.

Amanda screamed with the realization that The Field wasn't protecting them from the shape in the woods; it was *preparing* them for it.

A hand clapped over her mouth, and the dead, icy touch of the strange flesh sent shivers up and down her entire body.

21

BARNES COULDN'T DECIDE where to focus his attention. Straight ahead, this monstrous creature that shouldn't exist in the real world was lumbering toward them, its lengthy arms whipping about wildly as it moved clumsily through the tall grass. Not fast enough for something clearly hungry, but not slow either. It looked like a primate of sorts, only about twelve feet tall with eyes that were hardly human—animalistic orbs that glowed like hot ember—and long white tusks that belonged on a walrus and not this humanoid being. Its whiskered maw opened and closed, flashing deadly rows of serrated teeth.

He turned to his right to see Amanda struggling. Another being, one as oddly shaped as the thing from the forest, was positioned behind her, putting what looked like its hand over her mouth. The thing stood on two legs, its entire body covered in roots and caked in mud, twigs stuck out of the thing's back and chest. He knew the thing had once appeared as Brian, had granted him illusions of his death, the men that had so viciously slain him. The thing behind her *was* The Field. And, it was nothing like Phelps had imagined. It was not a relatively benign being that fed off a few people to keep them safe—no, it fed on people because that was what it did. Like all beings, this thing needed to eat and did so with gluttonous intent.

As for the thing in the forest closing the distance between them and *it,* Barnes didn't know what the fuck that terrible creature was, only that it was ugly and solely directed its attention on Phelps's mutilated remains.

The Field killed Phelps, Barnes thought, *and this thing is cleaning up after it. Sloppy seconds.*

Barnes ignored the bone-white creature with gangly features and faced the monster at Amanda's back. She'd driven a pair of scissors into its face, and the thing hadn't enough common sense to remove the shears from its muddy flesh. The scissors remained stuck where a mouth should have been. It bled mud from the injury, the syrupy brown substance leaking onto Amanda's head, showering her with an earthly filth.

Barnes searched the immediate area for a weapon and found nothing. He cursed Amanda for not letting him bring something along, anything he could have used for protection. She had gone with her instincts and had brought something for herself, and if she was willing to risk their lives for a pair of scissors, then why not go all out? Why not bring something bigger, more useful, why not let all of them carry?

Because... she had wanted to hide from it... The Field... she didn't want it to know... she didn't want us to know... for it to read her intent in our thoughts.

And apparently it hadn't, otherwise the all-powerful entity wouldn't have let her get close enough to harm it.

How'd she do it? How'd she hide from it?

He scanned the ground again. No available weapons of any kind. No branches he could substitute as a baseball bat. No sharp pieces of stone he could use as a makeshift knife. All he had was himself. His hands, his feet. His brain.

As the creature continued to hold onto Amanda's head, stealing the memories directly from the source, he noticed the tree—which had been naked and prepped for winter—had begun to bud, springing leaves of the greenish variety.

Whatever it was doing to Amanda, whatever it had done to them, the tree was reaping the benefits.

Maybe that's the thing's heart. Maybe that's its life source.

He didn't have anything else to go on, and the bone-white creature from the forest had already reached the outskirts of the flattened grass. Just as it entered the circle, making for Phelps's bloody, wrecked remains, Barnes decided he'd charge the earthly beast, grab the scissors from its head, and take to the tree. Do as much damage as he could before the thing opted to defend itself.

If he got that far. He half expected the monster (*monsters*) not to let him within ten steps of the blooming tree, but he had to try.

As the bone-white monstrosity hunched down on all fours and began feeding on Phelps's left arm, wedging flesh and bone between its pointy teeth and biting down, Barnes made his move. He sprinted toward Amanda and the thing that powered *The Field,* the thing responsible for the horrors at Spring Lakes.

He ran, and the thing turned on him.

Bellowed out.

Defended itself.

● ● ●

Her head felt like a melting rainbow; her memories were colors and they were all bleeding together, dripping on the ground before her. She saw each one pass through her before the thing that currently feasted on her lured the moments away. Her past was there, laid out before her, and then it wasn't. They'd become lost. Well, maybe not lost; lost implied she no longer knew where they were—but she knew. They belonged to The Field now, this thing that fed upon their lives, their memories, the good and the bad, and used their experiences to grow richer and prosper, to live another day or week or year or millennia so it could one day feed again.

It let her remember that.

Phelps had been gravely wrong about The Field. It wasn't protecting them. It was protecting itself.

"I'd have let you wander through the forest infinitely, but something tells me you three weren't going to give up searching for me. You'd hunt me until you found me; you'd bring more distractions and weapons, and that would bring more attention to me, and I can't be bothered with that kind of a nuisance. I've got a good thing going here. Much easier to dispatch you. Leave no trace of you for your friends to discover. But, first, allow me to drink and eat, dine upon your pasts."

From Amanda's mind, The Field stole another moment. This one of her fifth birthday party. Her parents had gotten her a pink Power Wheels Jeep. She had driven it around the driveway while the entire party clapped and laughed and cheered her on. Her grandfather had been there, laughing and clapping and cheering, had done all three with the biggest smile plastered to his face. Seeing it now made her want to retch, and she felt her gorge rise.

"Yes, that's it. Let me take your sicknesses and leave you with nothing. Your memories are cancer to you, aren't they? So tasty this disease, so delectable. I'll eat and drink them all from you, relieve you of their burden. Leave you with nothing. Your head will become a husk, a black starless expanse in your mind where no memories will grow. I will own your memories and I will own you."

"The sixty-niners..." Amanda was able to say, but that was about it. She still wanted to know how they fit into this puzzle. She had so many questions to ask The Field before it drained her, but she lacked the voice and energy to do so. It was hard to speak with your memories being sucked from your brain like a glass of milk through a straw.

"The sixty-niners give me power. There is power in numbers. Each universe has its own number, a common denominator of all things—some places it's seven, others it's nineteen or eleven. But here it's sixty-nine. It's not so often I feed on sixty-nine. They aren't too common at Spring Lakes. They are somewhat of a rarity, but I do come across them. Imagine my surprise when I discovered multiple humans age sixty-nine living no less than a mile from my den, a place I've lived for eternities. Their essence would procure my existence for a very long time. With their memories, I could go on hibernating for another eternity or two."

"What... are you... come from?" It ached to get the words out. A vacuum-like suck pulled on her brain, and she saw memories flash before her like a movie montage in fast motion.

The Field giggled in her ear. *"You humans are so obsessed with labels and information, wanting to know each and every thing. An infinite quest for knowledge. And that's the funny thing, isn't it? Because I'm a thing that has no name, has no label. I am what I am, and I don't seek anything beyond that. I feed, eat and drink, and that's my existence and there is no reason to investigate further. I come from the Dark Place where all things are born. You call me The Field and so that's what I am. I am The Field. This is my lair. A place of residence. Just like Spring Lakes is for some folk, this is where I sleep and prey on the minds of those around me, those sixty-nine. It's rare I feed outside those parameters, but I'll make special exceptions to protect myself, to ensure my survival. Like from you and your friends. Ensure you won't come back with more people, more disturbances. Trouble I do not need."*

Amanda's eyes drifted toward the thing that had pushed its way into the circle. A bone-white being that looked vaguely human, though its arms and legs were much too long and lacked muscle tone. Its limbs were oddly malformed, bent in all the wrong places, like a piece of plastic that had been warped by overexposure to an intense flame. Its skin was wrapped tightly to its skull, its powdery-white flesh smooth and wrinkle-free. Its cranium contained the blackest eyes she'd ever seen. Its jaw hung agape, the lower portion dropping an unrealistic distance, making it seem like the thing's face was made of rubber or some latex special effect. Its mouth was riddled with darkness, which was contrasted by the sharp ivory teeth that lined its gums both top and bottom. The teeth were also misshapen, curved at awkward angles and anatomically inefficient. She wondered how the thing could eat like that, but as it moved closer to the remains of Phelps's body, she figured she was destined to find out.

"Another creature from the Dark Place. I think it followed me here."

She didn't care about the creature, didn't care about The Field anymore. She cared about getting out of this thing alive, with or without her memories intact. Half of them The Field could keep; she didn't need them or want them. But the other half—like the images of the fig tree she'd already forgotten and left behind—she'd like to keep, hold onto them, remember them when she needed to, when she needed to remind herself of who she was and where she'd come from. Sometimes, memories are all we know about ourselves. Sometimes, the memories make us.

She turned away from the bone-white creature as it picked up one of Phelps's arms and began to gnaw on the flesh and muscle like a chicken wing. She saw Barnes approaching her, fast, a look of pure terror chiseled on his face.

She heard The Field let loose a terrible sound, a high-pitched whine that echoed across the tall grass, cut through the woods and beyond. Birds took flight into the sun-soaked sky. The wind shifted, temporarily numbing the scents of blood and certain death. The trees swayed like drunken soldiers finally home after a long assignment.

Amanda closed her eyes, believed those were the last sights and sounds of a world she no longer cared anything about. She prayed for a quick end.

22

THE LOOK THE Field directed at Barnes caused him to skid to a stop, made him rethink his strategy. There was no way he could get to the scissors without the thing taking a swipe at him. Even though the muddy, earthly creature was currently invested in the things Amanda Guerrero kept locked inside her mind, it wouldn't take much effort to turn and focus on him. And that was the last thing Barnes needed. He had wanted to surprise the thing, but The Field, seemingly aware of everything happening around it, had reacted in a way that had surprised him.

Barnes backed away, enough for The Field to continue its concentration on Amanda and her memory bank. As it withdrew from her, Barnes looked around once more, refusing to watch the other thing eat what was left of Phelps. He heard it munching on her meat and bones, the sounds of her remains squishing and crunching between its teeth, and that was enough to turn his stomach sideways, upside down—he surely didn't need the image to go along with it, though, as it stood, if he failed here today, maybe The Field would steal that image, relieve him of the burden of carrying around his last memory of Phelps and what her mistake had cost her.

Barnes spotted something he hadn't before. Something he'd seen when they had first arrived, the first time, but somehow had overlooked when he'd gone searching for a weapon only moments ago.

The stones.

Five of them, laid out in star-like fashion, each one representing a point.

How'd I miss that? It wasn't there before, seconds ago, he was sure of it. Or maybe it was and The Field, with its tricks and sensory magic, hadn't allowed him to see it. Maybe it had projected an image before him, rolled out a barren landscape like the background of a stage play, one without anything that could be used against it. But now, now that the thing was so entangled in feeding off Amanda's mind, maybe it had let its guard down some. Maybe he wasn't supposed to see those stones. Or, maybe if he bent down to pick up one, they'd slip right through his hand like an apparition. A ghost of what used to be there. Maybe there were no stones at all.

Barnes did bend down. He took one of the stones, about the size of a softball, and held it firmly with both hands.

All right, you son of a bitch, he thought, turning to the thing that had come from the earth, that had been born in this very field. He didn't know how old The Field was, only that it had been here long before mankind had been a twinkle in the universe's eye. He didn't know how he knew that or if it was true, but he couldn't ignore the suspicion that had been planted in his head by some unknown force. What they were dealing with, this cosmic entity, was as old as time itself. Maybe older.

Barnes charged forward, stone in hand, ready to strike.

It saw him coming again, but, this time, Barnes didn't hold back. He didn't allow it the chance of belting out another shrill noise; instead, he took the rock, leaped forward, and smashed The Field in the face. It knocked the thing back, separating it from its meal. The second its touch left Amanda's head, Barnes grabbed her by her wrist and pulled her away. He stepped in front of her to shield her from another attack, but The Field was still recovering from the blow to its head.

"Stay back," Barnes said, addressing both parties. The other living thing, the one resting in Barnes's periphery, was content on staying put, snacking on the bones of their co-worker, grinding her skeleton between its teeth. As it munched, it made noises, grunts and grumbles, suggesting it was very comfortable in its current position, and that it required no further sustenance, which didn't exactly bring Barnes any comfort. Knowing the thing was here was enough to keep him on guard.

"Are you okay?" Barnes whispered over his shoulder.

Amanda didn't respond. Not right away. But after a brief moment of her looking around, examining the field (and *The Field*) as if it were the first time she'd seen it, she shook her head and said, "Yes. Yes, I'm fine." Her voice was heavy with uncertainty.

"Good," he said, ignoring the possibility that she was lying. Barnes marched forward, figuring he could unpack everything else later. "I could use your help."

Amanda was slow, but she took his meaning. She scrambled over to the center of the pit, mindful that the beast feeding on Phelps's heap of a ruined body could abandon his meal at any time, and picked up the closest stone, immediately shifting on the offensive.

"Let's attack it at the same time," Barnes said, and then led the charge, leaving no time for her to question his judgment.

Amanda followed him, zero reluctance in her first step.

Barnes got there first, jumping and striking The Field's head. The rock crashed into the side of its mud-caked cranium, knocking the thing sideways. It stumbled. Amanda went for it at the knees, winding her arm back as if she were ready to deliver a fast-pitch softball. The sound of the stone connecting with the thing's bone reminded Barnes of snapping a twig over his thigh. The Field dropped, landing on both knees. Now its head was level with his chest, prime position for one final blow. Gritting his teeth, Barnes brought the stone over his head.

Don't.

The thing changed suddenly. He saw Brian kneeling there instead, his face puffed, swollen from the midnight beating that had ended his life. His eyes couldn't be seen behind the inflamed skin. His flesh had split in places, revealing the raw, red muscle beneath.

Barnes stopped immediately.

Don't hit me. Please.

Shit, he even sounded like Brian.

He was scared. His breathing was labored, his body taxed from the violent assault. One letter appeared on his neck.

F.

Please don't do that! Spittle spurted past his bloated lips.

Barnes felt tears trickle down his face.

No!

A.

"Stop it," Barnes heard himself mutter. "It's not real."

He felt Amanda's hand on his shoulder. It provided little comfort as the last letter split his boyfriend's flesh.

Brian howled louder than The Field had when Amanda had driven the scissors into its face.

"Not real," Barnes convinced himself.

Brian turned to him. "It's real, buddy. It's as real as you want it to be. It's as real as I can make it."

Something snapped in Barnes's chest; he could feel it. He no longer felt the sadness, that soul-emptying sorrow. There was regret—that would never leave—how he wished he could go back and take back all those hurtful insults, the ones he had thrown in Brian's face moments before his final departure. But the sadness was gone. The thing before him was not Brian. It was a shallow replica. A fraction of what the man had meant to him.

"You're not real," Barnes said again, and this time he felt numb. He brought the stone forward, cracking The Field on the top of its dome. When the skull broke open, squirting mud and other earthly fluid, Brian's visage vanished. Disappeared. The Field returned to its natural state, even though Barnes struggled to call whatever that thing truly was *natural.*

The impact rocked the thing, made another awful crunching noise, and Barnes knew that he'd fractured the thing's skull, if that indeed was what it had hidden behind the mud and hardened-earth shell it wore for a face. It sounded like someone stepping on a carton of eggs. He slammed the rock down again, this time forcing the thing onto its back. Amanda joined in this time, driving the stone down on its chest, crunching and cracking the brittle bones beyond its muddy filth of a body. Over and over again, they took turns striking The Field, breaking whatever they could.

Once the thing lay still, no longer breathing like an ordinary living creature, Barnes and Amanda stepped away, admiring what they'd accomplished. Behind them, they heard muscle being torn from bone, sounding like worn Velcro being ripped apart, and the slurping of their dissected friend's blood being lapped up by the hairless creature from the woods.

They turned on it. Its head rose from the good meal, its whiskered maw covered in glistening scarlet smears. Barnes and Amanda took one step forward, and the thing took one step back.

It's afraid of us, Barnes realized. The thing appeared to be a scavenger; not a hunter as they had previously thought. The Field had been the hunter, a thing that sought out food and aggressively pursued its quarry— but not this thing, this white, bald monster, whose gangly legs reminded him of a spider's, the way they were hinged in several places. No, not this thing that lived in the woods, or whatever void occupied the space beyond it. Some black, eternal expanse that harbored monstrosities and unseen things, horrible beasts that shouldn't exist—couldn't possibly exist—in the world they knew.

Yet, here the things were.

Barnes pretended to launch himself forward, a stutter step that was meant to test the thing's skittishness. The threat worked and the thing recoiled, fearing a frontal attack. Barnes and Amanda advanced on it, equipped with their mud-covered stones.

The bone-white creature reached out and grabbed one of Phelps's legs, bit down on it like a dog recovering its bone, and then retreated into the tall grass, slipping beyond the tree that had once sprouted green vibrant leaves. But now those green leaves had curled and crisped, reduced to the same color as the muddy earth. Barnes knew that was because of what they'd done to The Field, that they'd effectively exorcized it from this world, the world of the living. Barnes watched the bone-white creature make for the trees with surprising quickness. Amanda rushed past him, but Barnes reached out and grabbed her by the shoulder.

"Don't."

She shot him an *are-you-serious* glance, and he nodded.

"We'll never catch it. Besides, wherever it's going, I'm not sure we want to follow."

That statement brought a cool breeze that rippled across the straw grass and moved the dead branches of the lifeless tree that stood at the end of a dying field.

It took a moment, but she finally agreed, silently, nodding and resting her forehead on Barnes's chest, sobbing into the fabric of his dress shirt. He let her get as much of it out as she had to give, then backed her away from their friend's sickening remains with both hands on her shoulders.

"One more thing I think we need to do," he said and bent down. He tried his best to avoid what had become of Phelps, but in order to do what he needed, he couldn't help it. He concentrated on her body, the appendage-less mound, and dared not to look at the woman's face. He felt his emotions overcome him and he began to cry, his eyes filling with a blurriness that he was somewhat thankful for. He felt around the lower half of her, and, ten seconds later, he located her back pocket, the place she'd kept her lighter, the one he'd borrowed and used to smoke many of her cigarettes.

Once he had retrieved it, he stood up immediately, walked over to The Field, kneeling down and grabbing a fistful of straw grass. Then he stood over the crumpled, ruined mass that was The Field, and lighted the straw grass, watched as the flames took to the source. Once the grass was burning, he dropped the makeshift torch onto The Field's carcass. Then he bent down and gathered more grass and straw, lighting it as well. Amanda came over and provided a barrier between the flames and the wind, blocking out the earthly currents that tried to sabotage their final task.

After a few minutes, The Field was burning good and steady, progressing with each moment. Flames climbed higher. Raged. The turbulent black smoke reached for the darkening skies, which, in turn, brought the fire-starters instant satisfaction. The combined putrid stink of the fire and mud and whatever lay beneath it didn't bother them.

Together, they watched the fire. They watched the sky. Darkness settled over The Field, a darkness that would end and, eventually, bring new light.

23

THE WALK BACK to Spring Lake took less time than anticipated. When they emerged from the woods, Amanda expected bedlam. Police activity, sirens and bouncing lights, but there was nothing of the sort. The Spring Lake Assisted Living Facility sat in the pale purple glow of the dying afternoon, looking abandoned. And it pretty much had been; there wasn't anyone left inside except a few souls, the sixty-niners, Kim Charon and her small crew. Two of them, she noticed, were outside leaning on the railing.

The Lawyers.

Hatterman and Hart.

One of them, Hatterman, was kneeling down, holding onto the railing for support, as if the world were a boat that had hit turbulent waters. The other kept his hand on his partner's back, comforting him. Over what, Amanda hadn't the slightest. All data suggested that, since they'd dispatched The Field, everything should return to normal. The sixty-niners should be cured from whatever hold The Field had over them, whatever methods it had used to paralyze them while it leeched off their memories. After all, her own memories had come flooding back to her once Barnes had set fire to its corpse. She could remember everything now—her grandfather's depravity, the fig tree, the pink Power Wheels—so, if that was true, then it stood to reason the others would be okay.

Then why did Hatterman look like he'd just been sucker-punched in the gonads?

Barnes escorted her up the steps, making sure she didn't lose her balance. Once at the top, the lawyer who wasn't kneeling spotted them, turned his attention away from his friend.

"Don't go in there," Hart said, his voice shaky, clearly panicked. "The police will be here soon."

Barnes and Amanda ignored his request and hustled inside. They heard the man make another plea, begging them not to look around, but they tuned him out, headed down the hall.

Jogging now, they made for Kim's office. It was slightly ajar, and the way it had almost been pulled shut set off an alarm in Amanda's head. Barnes got in front of her, made his way to the door first. He pushed it open.

Amanda backed away, shielding her eyes from the sight, though it was hardly the worst thing she'd witnessed that day.

Kim, dangling from the end of a garden hose, hanged in the center of the office. Her chair had fallen over, lay motionless beneath her feet.

"Shit," Barnes said, raising his eyes to the fan that the woman's weight had pulled from the ceiling. They'd been too late, clearly, and Kim Charon had successfully committed suicide.

There was no way to know that she'd do it, Amanda thought. She put a hand on Barnes's back, readied herself to tell him such, and then he shut the door, closing it all the way until they heard the latch bolt click into place.

He turned to her.

"We should check on them," Amanda said. "The sixty-niners."

Barnes let her take the lead. He followed her down the hall and to the left. She went directly to Manuel Renteria's room.

She turned the handle, opened the door with her shoulder. She poked her head in first, had herself a look around before committing to entering. She saw the sixty-nine-year-old man sitting in his chair, much where she'd left him.

His eyes were open. Blinking. At the sound of her stepping into the room, he glanced up. Toward her. At her. He was conscious, aware of what was going on around him.

"Mr. Renteria?" Amanda asked the man who, now, looked nothing like her *abuelo.*

"Yes?" he asked, no evidence of confusion in his voice.

"Are you... feeling okay?"

"Fine. Quite fine."

He didn't look like her grandfather, not in the slightest. He looked like his own person, a man she'd never met before. Someone she wouldn't recognize in the streets if their paths crossed. Someone she wouldn't mistake for a friend, a relative, an immediate family member. Manuel Renteria was his own self and seeing him as he truly was brought a warm, toasty feeling to her limbs. To her soul.

"Glad to hear it," she told him.

"Could I have a glass of water, sweetheart? I'm parched."

Amanda smiled at him. "You can have whatever you want." She kissed the crown of his head.

Barnes had walked away from the room to check on the others. When he came back, he told her, "They're all fine. No memory of anything. It's like they... just woke up from a dream or something."

"A nightmare is more likely."

"No," he said. "Just a dream. They're all fine. More than fine, actually. A lot of them are lucid and making sense. Talking about things that are... well, that are normal. Some of the nurses are quite shocked. Said this is the most normal they've ever seen them. Hardly exhibiting any signs of dementia."

Amanda nodded. "Good. That's... that's really good."

Outside, sirens whistled, getting closer and closer. The authorities would be there momentarily. Then the real fun would begin. The explaining. The lies. It would take some good ones to make sense of all this.

"What's our story?" Barnes asked. "What do we tell them?"

Amanda shrugged. "We could tell them the truth."

Barnes sighed, and never said if he agreed or not.

Amanda's phone interrupted the moment. "Yes," she answered. "It's Guerrero."

"Amanda," said the voice belonging to her boss, Denny Cohen, one of the team members who should have been here by now. *"Amanda, I'm so sorry we were never able to meet you. We've had issues all day. You wouldn't believe it. First the plane, then there was a mix-up at the car rental place, and—well, suffice it to say, we're still on our way."*

"I see."

"Tell me you've found something. Anything as to what it is?"

"Actually, I think our work here is done."

Cohen took a pause. *"It is?"* He sounded surprised. *"You sounded so panicked earlier. So perplexed. I mean, I'm damn glad you figured it out. What was it? Brain-eating bacteria like you thought?"*

"Yes," she said, and almost smiled. "Yeah, something like that."

"Well, that's great. Because we're gonna need you in California."

Barnes and Amanda looked at each other. The doors at the end of the hall swung open, and a parade of police officers and emergency first responders funneled inside.

"What's in California?"

"A woman, sixty-nine years young, never woke up this morning in Sacramento. But she's alive, all her vitals are

registering. Just... paralyzed. Also, she's pre-Alzheimer's, just like the fine folks you apparently just saved."

Amanda's throat clenched. She couldn't respond. Her voice locked up.

"Amanda? You still there?"

Barnes took the phone from her. "Cohen, it's Barnes. Listen, things are getting a little hectic over here. There have been some... fatalities."

"Fatalities?"

"Yes, Kim Charon, the facility's director—she... took her own life."

"She what?"

"Yeah, I know. I don't know why, but things—as you can imagine—are getting a little crazy. Phelps is also..." Amanda shook her head. He improvised. "...she's missing. Can't find her anywhere. I'm sure she'll turn up, but it's unlike her to disappear. Look, this California thing—can you stick someone else on it? We're gonna be tied up for at least the afternoon."

Cohen paused as if he expected Barnes to change his tune. *"I'll see what I can do. Atlanta wants a full report ASAP, though. That way they can get it out to Cleveland, Detroit, and Portland too."*

Amanda's nerves took another shot. She suddenly found herself against the wall, sliding down it.

"Why? What's... what's happening in those places?" asked Barnes, his voice nearly failing him.

"Haven't you guys been checking your emails?" Cohen asked, sounding a little aggravated. *"Damn thing is happening in several places. All the same symptoms. Sixty-nine-year-olds. Looking dead but still showing a heartbeat. All previously exhibiting traits of Alzheimer's. Dementia. I don't know what the hell is happening but if you three solved it in New Jersey, then I'm guessing you have a pretty good idea. So yeah, we're gonna need those reports and fast."*

"I see," Barnes said through his teeth.

Amanda felt lightheaded. Weak. Her world swam. She planted herself on the floor.

Barnes hung up the call, handed her the phone. The iPhone slipped through her fingers and hit the ground, hard. The screen cracked. She hardly cared.

Next came the wave of police officers and medical personnel. After a few minutes, she stood up—with Barnes's help—and pushed her way through the crowd, ignoring the onslaught of "ma'ams" and "are you okays."

"I need air," was her answer to everyone and everything.

She stumbled out into the dying light. The lawyers were sitting on the back of an ambulance having their vitals taken. The parking lot was littered with police and emergency vehicles. Overhead, a news chopper circled the area. Beyond the parking lot, several people with cameras and microphones were climbing out of vans.

But she ignored them all and stared straight into the tiny entrance into the woods.

Her grandfather was there. Smiling. Waving her on.

She waved and smiled back, watched as he slipped behind the foliage, dragging his awkwardly bent appendage out of sight. His entire backside was charred to a crisp.

She knew where he was headed—The Field. Where he lived and breathed.

And she, of course, would have to follow.

69

MISSY TISDALE BROUGHT Rachel Downey a cup of tea, set it down on the table in front of her. Rachel looked up from her game of solitaire and accepted the tea with a smile. She thanked Missy and returned to her game, taking a moment to remember exactly where she'd left off. Missy pointed out a potential next move, then left her to it.

Next, she patrolled the common area, asking the guests if they needed anything; tea, water, a soda pop; whatever their hearts desired, Missy would bring it.

After she finished with her rounds, she headed to the break room. It wasn't even noon yet and a third cup of coffee called to her. As she loaded the community Keurig with a pumpkin spice K-cup, she felt a shadow approach, fall over her like a cloud on an otherwise bright and sun-shiny day.

"Missy?" a small, sorrowful voice asked.

Missy pressed the start button and turned around. "Yes, Emily?"

"I'm afraid I have some bad news."

The expression on the young CNA's face drove a spike through her heart. "Oh god, who is it?"

"Miss G."

"Christ." Missy bit her lip. "When did she pass?"

"Just now. Maybe in the last hour."

Missy nodded, gripping the counter for support. She felt unusually unsteady.

"I know how close you were."

Missy cleared her throat. "She was a good woman."

"Alice wanted me to find you, in case you wanted to say goodbye."

Using her thumb, Missy wiped a teardrop from her eyelash. "Yeah, I'd like that very much."

Emily held her hand as they strolled down the hallway, no hurry in their pace. The whole way there, Missy felt lightheaded. Like a piece of her had been taken, forcefully and without mercy. It was a strange way to feel about someone she'd only known for a year, but Emily was right—she'd grown close to the woman. She had made her laugh, had told her riveting stories, treated her as if she were family. It was the mother/daughter relationship Missy had never had with her *real* mom, the one who'd raised her, if she could call it such. If spending all afternoon scoring drugs and all-night shooting junk into her veins counted as parenting.

"You okay?" asked Emily. They were outside the woman's door now. Alice, the head CNA, was waiting there with two other nurses. They looked sad. It was a sudden loss, one that would be felt from the top on down.

"Yeah, I'll be fine."

Emily helped her to the door.

"Take as long as you like, dear," Alice told her.

More tears came; she couldn't help it. When she walked into the dorm, she felt something heavy drape over her, as if she'd walked into a sauna and the weight of the steam had folded over her like a lead curtain. As if there was something alive in here, with her; although, there shouldn't have been anything.

(dead)

How can she be dead?

Sixty-nine was too young. *Way* too young.

Missy sat down across from the woman who'd died sitting in her chair, her head tilted back, staring at the ceiling. She held a pen in her hand. A note had been left on the desk. Missy stared at it, wondering why she'd scribbled down two numbers the moment before she succumbed to death's touch.

6.

9.

Sixty-nine?

"I'm so sorry, Miss Guerrero," Missy said, reaching out and taking her cold, freezing hand. Her flesh felt like an ice cube.

(dead)

Something moved in the woman's throat. Her flesh danced. Missy jumped back, shrieked. The other nurses quickly filled the room, each whispering their concerns, asking questions Missy didn't have answers for.

Are you okay?

What happened?

Is everything all right?

Instinctively, Missy reached out, felt for the carotid artery in Miss Guerrero's neck. She knew she had found it when she felt the woman's pulse.

"Amanda?"

Nothing.

Still.

Frozen.

(dead)

"Oh my god, I think she's alive."

Sixty-nine.

Too young to die.

ACKNOWLEDGEMENTS

Much love to my wife, Ashley, who keeps me sane. Thanks to Matt Hayward who made this book look nice and pretty with his expert formatting skills. I salute Tim Feely and Lydia Capuano for beta reading this beast. Of course, my editor, Jenny Adams, who makes me sound smarter than I actually am. All the Bookstagrammers and book reviewers who have liked, shared, and posted about my work - y'all are the best and I wouldn't be here without your support. THANK YOU. If you're reading this, then a special thanks goes out to you as well.

Until we meet again, friends.

Tim Meyer
6/14/2019

ABOUT THE AUTHOR

TIM MEYER dwells in a dark cave near the Jersey Shore. He's an author, husband, father, podcast host, blogger, coffee connoisseur, beer enthusiast, and explorer of worlds. He writes horror, mysteries, science fiction, and thrillers, although he prefers to blur genres and let the stories fall where they may.

You can follow Tim at https://timmeyerwrites.com OR like his Facebook page here:

www.facebook.com/authortimmeyer